CREEP
WITH A CAMERA

KYLE YADLOSKY

MONTAG

First Montag Press E-Book and Paperback Original Edition June 2017

Montag Press
ISBN: 978-1-940233-41-3
Cover photo © Bewakoof
Interior and co design © 2017 Niall Gray
Editor & Managing Director – Charlie Franco

A Montag Press Book
www.montagpress.com
Montag Press
1066 47th Ave. Unit #9
Oakland CA 94601 USA

Montag Press, the burning book with the hatchet cover, the skewed word mark and the portrayal of the long-suffering fireman mascot are trademarks of Montag Press.

Printed & Digitally Originated in the United States of America
10 9 8 7 6 5 4 3 2 1

Creep With A Camera is an unsettling, uncomfortable, unnerving journey. After reading the final word, I wasn't sure if I wanted to take a shower or journey out into the bowels of the nearest city, in the middle of the night, just to smell the grime and see the filth. Filled with tales that are both lurid and grotesque, this book is a dirty pool, but forget nervously dipping your toes into it, to truly experience it, you have to dive in and swim.

— Jonathan R. Rose, author of *Carrion*

Creep with a Camera is a visceral, photo-laden fugue, shot through the lens of an obsessive, damaged soul as he embarks on a series of ritualistic, risqué adventures. Yadlosky has fashioned a philosophically perverse and darkly humorous tale, focusing his first-person F-stop on a world of depraved beauty and horror. This is a creepy and compulsive debut novel, a *Peeping Tom* for the digital age.

— C.M. Muller, editor of *Nightscript*

For my parents.

Jennifer and Howie

Let's call her Jennifer. She looks like a Jennifer. Green army coat sewn with generals' patches running down to a pleated red skirt, purple tights underneath hugging smooth legs that fall into brown clogs, and her brown hair lying against her back. She's a mannequin in a window, a model in a photo. A cutout from an L.L Bean catalogue. She's not real, not a person, so I can name her whatever I want. I can make her whomever I want. And so I decide she's the kind of girl who doesn't match on purpose, who fits in so well that she has to go out of her way so she won't fit in anymore. A hard life, I'm sure.

Pools of water glisten on the sidewalk under nightlight. I have to watch my step on the slick concrete, so I don't splash. My steps run smooth, my body close to the walls. I'm wallpaper. I'm always wallpaper. The city has that wet dog smell of rain still hanging in the air. I don't mind. The alleys that I walk reek with worse scents.

Slippery though it may be, I won't fall on the sidewalk, but I could fall for Jennifer. I mean, she would need to know me first, and I would need to know her real name, obviously. I'm not a psychopath, but I could fall for her. I can see us making shy smiles and casual conversation. Our hands touching. Our lips touching. Bliss in every way. All fantasy. I don't need to know what she's like as a human to fantasize about loving her.

But love won't happen. Not tonight. If she saw me she would scream, run from me, find the police. And they would surely rescue her with guns and bullets that would tear me down, the street soaking in my blood. An ugly noise would rattle out my throat, and I'd be left to die in the gutter. My soul wandering the sewers with the rats and crocodiles. Sad stuff. Not the worst thing to ever happen to a person. But still.

Someday women will line up for me, no matter how I look or sound or smell. I just have to struggle through until then.

This Jennifer winds her way through street after street, moving farther to the back of the city where the number of late night revelers lessens to a degree that makes me look increasingly suspicious. I have to act more suspiciously to remain unseen. I press against corners, lean up against dumpsters, my head tilted down, pretending to smoke a cigarette I don't even have. My empty fingers open to scissors, blowing out the steam of my own breath instead of smoke.

Eventually she finds such secluded places that there's no one around anymore to catch how much my miming skills have developed in such a short time.

Jennifer struts her purple legs to a red Jaguar Type F sitting alone in a parking lot bathed under light so harsh it could be on stage. A red show car out in a place like this makes no sense, anyway. Maybe it all has been set up for me, for my eyes only.

I can't make out anything inside. I set my shoulder bag on the ground and assemble my camera while the side door thunks open and shut.

It's a good camera. A Canon. One with those long lenses for seeing things you're afraid to get too close to. Like lions or bigfoot, or even people sometimes. I bought it, so I could see them better. People that is. Not to take secret pictures or anything. I'm not a creep.

I snap a few photos. No flash. Just a wide aperture and slow shutter. I'm not stupid.

She sits in the red car on brown seats next to a jock-type guy, a bro, who chews on his fingernails as she speaks. He has a weird nose. I'll call him Howie. Howie is kind of a dumb name, and he looks kind of dumb. Maybe I'm just jealous that he has a girl in his car, but that's his life, not mine.

I don't have a car.

I can't hear what they are saying. They mouth secrets behind the windshield. In my mind I make up their words as my camera glides from one face to the next, picking up their back and forth. They're just models here for me, posing, moving, giving the impression of life. They're posing to give me the shots I need, so I can become the man I want to be.

Howie rubs his jaw. "Hey, babe. What took you so long?"

Jennifer's lips open and close, kisses stamped on each word. "I had to walk. Why didn't you come get me?"

Seriously, she's right. What kind of person would wait in his car almost a mile away for a woman to come to him? What an asshole. I don't like him already.

Howie turns his head up. My camera catches the high def detail of every hair twisting in his nostrils. I snap a picture. His mouth opens and closes. "Let's just fuck, you dumb bitch."

What a piece of shit.

I can see Jennifer grab his thigh, and Howie turns his head again. He presses his lips shut. She kisses him on his chin. He lifts a thick hand and holds it to her shoulder. I snap a photo of this. Not that I'm going to sell it to *Life* or anything.

He opens the driver's side door and slams it shut. He paces on the asphalt, his hands shoved into his pockets, breathing smoke and looking up at the sky. I turn my camera eye to Jennifer. She sits in the car awhile, looking dead ahead. Her eyes wide and empty. I could mistake her face with its lipstick and off-kilter hair for that of a sex doll's. She sits rigid, falling deep inside herself. She swallows, closes her eyes, and opens the car door.

I snap a picture of her standing on one side of the car, holding the open door. Howie stands on the other, under the light staring up at the sky. Each looks in the opposite direction, off the edges of the frame. Jennifer fills the dark side, Howie the light. They both blow steam.

Jennifer's voice starts again, but it's too low, too caught in hoarse mumbles for me to catch. I take apart the camera. Working with practiced speed while crouching in the alley, I set it back in the bag. I could hear what they say, if I were closer or if my ears were just a bit better, so my hand fishes into another pocket for my long-range microphone. I snap the pieces out, screw them together, glancing back up at the two pacing figures murmuring under the moonlight, and adjust the headphones over my ears. I bought this device, because a human's ears can only hear so much. The fact that the device records everything they say has nothing to do with it; that's just the way the Japanese manufacture it.

I raise the mic and hear their voices for the first time.

"I don't know what you want me to say," Jennifer chokes like through a gust of swallowed smoke.

"I don't know why I came out here." Howie's voice is smoother but runs a sharp trace of anger.

"I needed help," Jennifer says biting her fist.

"Do you really want help?"

Jennifer sighs, pushes her hair back, looks at him. "Of course, I do."

"Then, what were you trying to do?"

"Oh, come on. The way you look at me."

"I've never looked at you like that." Howie's voice rumbles a coming storm.

"Oh, come on," Jennifer presses. "You spied. I know you did." She struts to the front of the car, sits on it, watching Howie's back while he paces.

"I never spied," Howie grunts. "My friends spied, but I didn't."

"Oh, okay," she teases.

He throws her a glance. Pure malice. This chills her. She looks at her waist. He looks at the stars again.

He clears his throat. "What do you need?"

"A little support," she whimpers.

He flips a hand, turns to her. "You got me out here in the middle of the night, don't you."

"Money, a bed."

"I can give you some cash, for a hotel. But what will you do after that?"

She shrugs. "I might blow that money if you don't stick around to watch how I spend it."

He steps a half-foot toward her. "You should go to the church."

Here, she starts to weep. She buries her face in her hands. My headphones crackle with her sobs. My heart breaks for this girl. This is a play, a Marlon Brando movie. The sounds and voices, the lines so well delivered, are all present, so I can capture the drama I decide is here. This heroine, this porcelain girl destroyed by her own needs and damaged by some Polo sweater dickhead.

Howie sits next to her. He drops an arm across her shoulders, and she leans into him.

"I'm sorry," she whispers almost too low for my mic to catch. I shift where I crouch and try to lift it higher. Pooling water seeps into my shoes and soaks my socks. I curl my toes and uncurl them to keep them warm. The asshole chews on his lips, just watching her.

Eventually, he runs a hand down her hair to the small of her back. You dog, Howie. Jennifer notices. She reaches, drops a hand on his shoulder and cranes her neck toward his. Their mouths open. Their lips touch.

Howie jumps from the hood, wipes his mouth, shakes his head. Instant regret. What I'd give to be in his place. I wouldn't squander her offer, that's for sure. But isn't that how we all feel, watching a drama? What we would do differently, how we would change the plot. But spectators can only ever spectate. It's our curse?

"Don't do that." Again, he rumbles thunder.

Jennifer leans forward on the car, a model, holding her legs as her pale hands slide up her calves, leaning in to show the cleft of her breasts. She pushes her upper arms together for enhanced cleavage. She grins. Her teeth crooked. "You liked it."

"Stop it."

"Just say it."

He whips his foot against the pavement, splashing water, ringing.

"I'm your brother!" He shouts thunder that claps and rings and shoots down my alleyway. The mic explodes with feedback, making ever cell in my ear scream in agony as it dies. I pull the headphones off, gritting my teeth, and try to take in the silence. I shake my head, close my eyes. My ears still ring.

The car peels out.

I look over the trashcan and watch his red car throw water to its sides, red tail lights glowing, as it winds down the empty street and turns into darkness.

Jennifer stands under that single light in the empty parking lot for a while. In her hand she clutches a wad of cash. A vacant look holds her eyes again. Her face points in my direction. I'd be caught; she'd be staring right at me, if she weren't staring so deeply into herself. Good thing for me. I guess.

Her eyes move. She blinks crying, looks at the money clenched in her fist. She breathes smoke and shoves the wad into her coat pocket. Jennifer scans the parking lot one last time and starts her walk back into the city's beating heart.

I keep behind her as she walks sidewalks that run with as much water as her face. She sniffs and rubs the snot and tears on the sleeve of her coat. I press to the walls. I'm bricks; I'm mortar.

We cross into more populated streets where the drunks are still laughing, reel and fall in the gutter. One man tries to hold his girlfriend up and whispers in her ear. She lets loose a cackle that draws nearby eyes. I could be following them tonight, but I chose Jennifer. I'm happy I did.

Her back grows toward me as I stalk closer. More people pack around me, and my comfort rises. I walk a little faster. She sways and stumbles, still crying. Some eyes turn toward us. At this point I tail close enough behind her that people might think we're walking together. Maybe they think we fought, and she's pushing ahead with anger while I can only follow and wait for her to forgive me. Maybe her mother just died, and she wants to be alone, but I'm trying to console her. No one knows us, so we can be whatever they want us to be. These thoughts make me happy.

I watch myself step beside her, drape my coat around her shoulders. She hugs it over herself, blinks tears, flashes a shy smile. I introduce myself. She tells me her name is Jennifer, and that makes me grin, because she looked just like a Jennifer. We both laugh. I hug an arm around her back but hesitate to pull her in. She flashes me a look, a thin but needing smile, so I pull her, and she falls. She holds me as we walk up the street, and she tells me she has some money; she asks if I'd care to share a hotel room with her. She doesn't want to spend the night alone. I tell her I'm a gentleman, and I'd be happy to share the room with her, but only because she needs someone around. And she takes me to a motel where she can only afford one bed. And even though I said I was a gentleman, she rewards me for my efforts.

I guess it could happen. She's certainly ready to go and none too picky about who she goes with. I could try it. At least. I could say something to her. I could step from the shadows. I could peel myself from the walls.

But I don't. This isn't a romance story, and I certainly have nothing to offer her in ways of looks, charm, or obvious sexual prowess. I'm not that kind of man, yet. I stay three steps behind her as she wanders bewildered to the foot of a towering cathedral with double doors as big as the bottoms of ships.

She watches the doors, blinking tears and sniffing snot. She steps up a stair. Then, stops. She looks back. She turns from the church and wanders back to the sidewalk, another three blocks to a main road. Cars and tractor trailers rattle and roar. I don't need to worry about how heavy my footfalls sound with the growling engines, spinning tires, and splashing puddles overshadowing any noise. She wanders to a dingy motel. It smells worse than the wet dog air around it.

I stop and stand on the sidewalk. There are too many lights shining on its parking lot, on its buildings, and too few cars for me to safely melt into the background. Jennifer marches in, feet ticking on every step of the pavement, toward the front office. I could still catch her. My foot jerks an inch. I have some money. I could still have her. I could still make her mine. Or at least try.

But she steps inside before I make up my mind, and when she comes out she has a key. There's nothing I can do. I can't walk up to her, ask her if she needs help, offer her my coat. She's almost inside, and I'd just come off as desperate. Desperate for a place to stay.

And if there's one thing I'm not, it's desperate.

I watch her a while longer from the dark. The dark only breaks with the headlights of the cars speeding behind me. She fumbles with her key, fits it in the lock, turns it, and pulls herself in. I walk to her door after she's inside. The curtains are drawn. She can't see me. I assemble my camera and flash a shot of her door. Her room number is G 18. If I played bingo, I would only take cards with that number.

I press my ear to the door and hear her murmuring inside. On the phone, I guess. I could knock. Maybe she still needs company. But I don't, I can't, I won't. I'm not that kind of guy.

It starts to really rain.

I pull my hands into my pockets and march against the cold downpour. Trucks blast by, throwing waves of water at me that soak my coat. I shiver and try to ignore it. I hold my equipment bag under my coat and away from the street. I don't care what happens to my body as long as my tools survive.

Ahead, the lights of a vehicle blazes a white light that blinds and burns streaks of color onto my sight. I lift a hand, and the car takes my cue. The headlights dim as the high beams are turned down. I see it. A red classic, brown interior, a strange-nosed man driving inside. I watch him shoot down the main road and turn in toward the motel, and I smirk to myself.

Howie, you are a dog.

Richard

He looks like the kind of man for whom life was made up. Hugo Boss suit pressed to his skin, his blond hair gelled back from a tower of forehead, streaked with white. Bags hung under his eyes, and he wears enough grizzle to let everyone know he's perpetually unhappy. He's that kind of practiced clean. The kind you imagine honing since childhood—though not by choice, of course. He was born into money, went to an Ivy League school, and took over the family shop after his old man's last heart attack. Now he sits alone and drinks at a back table in one of the city's middle-class bars. A clean and quiet place. A place where the old professionals go to drink until they forget enough to stomach the return home.

He's upper-class decay, the abortion of an American Dream twisted like a wire hanger. A picture of the unhappiness of easy success. He was set here for me to notice, for me to watch, for me to follow.

I see a woman approach him at the bar. She struts in that way women do when they know the men have money. Sauntering to his side she runs her hand across his shoulder, and without waiting for his invite, sits next to him. She leans her velvet head to his ear and whispers something. It would be suspicious for me to pull out a recording device in this, a crowded bar, so I don't hear what she whispers. I can't even read their lips to make a guess. All I know is that it involves her tongue from the way she flashes it across her teeth when she pulls her head from his.

He slowly mouths four words that I can see, words that coil that woman's tongue back into her head and turns her tits from his face. Head high, she saunters away from the bar without a second glance.

"I have crippling aids."

"I have a ball gag."

"I have anal beads."

Whatever he said, it went along the lines of "I have something bad."

Before standing, stretching his back, patting down his jacket and pants, and walking from the bar in the measured steps of an actor practicing his blocking, he drinks a while longer in his solitude. On his way out he mutters some words to himself, and paws up a promotional matchbook lying on the counter.

Following, I keep an easy distance from him. Far enough to be seen by anyone in the bar glancing past as my own man on my own mission but not so far that when Roger—I'm calling this one Roger—swings the door shut behind him, that I can't breeze it open and catch his gait further down the street.

He walks a block off to a parking lot. One where you have to pay. One with tall walls and gates and guards. The status symbol of parking lots. The kind of place where a well-to-do man like him can feel secure that his vehicle is free from any groping hands or prying eyes, from any scum or shit streaks—and from people like me. The machine scans his parking ticket at the entrance, so the door will beep open, and he enters. Me, I walk around to where the cars pull in and affect being in a hurry, running past the booth attendants flashing something that could be mistaken for a parking ticket if it's blurry enough. I'm banking on the hope that they won't care enough to track me down, and almost all of the time no one really cares as much as you or he would hope they would.

I catch Roger strolling down D block. He straightens his hair, coughs into his hand and smells the air on his hand. Not liking what he smells, he reaches into his coat and pops a mint, its crunch echoing between the concrete walls. He swallows, breathes again, smells and pops another mint. He continues down the parking lot crunching the candy between his teeth.

Turning down E block, Roger fishes out of his pocket a steel ring jingling with keys to what I'm sure are several cars and a couple houses, perhaps a vacation homes, and a private boat. He thumbs a button on a fat and long key, and the lights ahead of him flash, its horn bleating once. The car is a black Mercedes. Naturally. Roger straightens his hair a final time before approaching it. It is the kind of car you have to work to impress. Need to look good, or the engine doesn't start.

I skulk low between cars an aisle across from his, a tall Range Rover saving my knees from crouching behind the tight sports cars and vintage wagons. I set my shoulders to the back of the vehicle and peer toward Roger's black sedan. I unpack my bag and lift out the camera. I shoot the well-kept car. I don't know how I'll keep up with him once he climbs in. Most likely I won't, but that's the spirit of the night. Maybe soon late night public transit will become more popular with more people, then I won't have to lose as many subjects to their drives home.

I lift the camera to my eye and zoom the lens toward the car, and I see something. There's a girl, maybe fourteen, sitting in the passenger's side seat, her eyes glued to her phone. She beats at the screen with her fingers and frowns. Her eyes look to Roger briefly before returning to the electronic glow.

Roger leans in. He knocks on the window. She glances up to him. He throws her a little wave. She looks back to her phone, raising her shoulders toward her cheeks. He knocks again. "Come on," he says.

She rolls down her window, looks him full in the face with a set of eyes that don't believe a word he has to offer. "I know. I'm late," he grumbles. She watches him, and he shifts, holding his collar and looking down to think. He licks his lips before he keeps speaking. "I'm sorry about that."

"How drunk are you?" she asks. "On a scale of one to ten."

He shrugs.

"You're a shit dad."

"Sorry."

I catch the look of defeat that hits his eyes in the snap of the camera shutter. He might not be drinking because his parents gave him the life that he has, because he had to follow in the footsteps of their career. Maybe he drinks because he has to follow in their footsteps as parents. Those being the four words that will turn any piece of tail in a bar.

"I have a daughter."

"Can you drive?" the girl asks, eyes back on her phone.

"I think so," Roger mutters.

"Do you need me to drive?"

"No. We can't do that again. It's illegal, dangerous."

She laughs to herself, and shakes her head.

"As opposed to what? Driving drunk?"

"At least that'll be on me."

"And who's going to take me home? Who will be there when I get home?"

She watches his wide eyes and working jaw for a while. He moves his shoulders, shuffles his feet. His mouth works its way into making a sentence.

"Your mother."

"She's worse than you."

Rich people shouldn't reproduce. Spoiled, entitled brats pop out of every golden vagina filled with enough pearls to spit something up. Snotty, gum chewing, cell phone playing, pregnant getting, making more rich sons of bitches, brats. It's not right. The poor, on the other hand, make just the right kind. There's something about being impoverished that teaches a person dignity, respect. And the young women it produces. Desperation will take a girl a long way. Like a flea wrestling through the matted hair of this city, those women are the only women I need.

"She's not so bad," Roger starts.

"She's an awful cunt." His daughter holds her eyes onto her phone.

"Don't say—"

"Cunt. Cunt. Cunt. You know she is."

Roger scratches the back of his neck, as his daughter rolls up the Benz's window.

Entitled little asshole. Every single one of them. If the only way I could ever fuck would be to put one inside one of those women—I'd probably do it—but afterwards I'd kill myself. For sure.

Roger walks to the back of the car and pops the trunk. His daughter sighs and slides down the chair, lifting the phone directly in front of her face.

As I watch, something shuffles past the corner of my eye—a dash of white from inside the dark of the rover. I turn my head just to catch the scrap of a small dog bounding over the chairs, scraping its paws against the leather interior, and throwing itself into the back of the vehicle where I've hidden myself. The dog jumps up and stands on its back legs, scraping its paws against the back window. It whimpers. I try to duck out of its sight. This only makes the little mutt scrapes and whimpers harder. What's with rich people leaving kids and pets in their cars?

The pooch pulls its lips back, shows its teeth, and a growl bubbles up in its throat. It then opens its mouth and lets a screeching bark loose. My shoulders still pressed up against the vehicle shiver at the noise. The girl drops her phone down into her lap and looks across the parking lot. Her eyes catch mine, and I dive down behind a little red convertible next to the range rover. The dog barks again, as I pull myself farther down the aisle on my hands and knees, until I reach a green sport scar. I have to hunch very low to stay hidden behind it.

When I get a chance to look at the Mercedes again, the girl is back to playing on her phone. I can't see Roger from that angle. I have to slink across the aisle and between cars to the back where he is still hunches into the trunk. He has placed a red oil jug next to his leg. He flips up and holds out a stained rag. I snap a shot of him. Holding the rag to his nose he looks ahead through the car window at the back of his daughter's head.

He unscrews the gas cap and sets the rag inside.

Roger flashes the pack of matches that he swiped from the bar and presses them against his lips. He closes his eyes for a moment, holding his breath. He closes the trunk, sets the matches on the back of the car, and he lifts the gas jug.

The stench flows harsh and fast that I can smell it from where I am. The thick liquid slicks the hair back on his head. It plasters his lips and eyes shut. He soaks his suit jacket, shirt, tie, and pants. He shakes the last of it out onto his shoes. His palm slaps the back of the car, fumbling for the pack of matches. His fingers wrap it, and his stuttering hands twitch to pop the pack open. He holds one up. It trembles in his unsteady grip. He pivots, and swipes it blindly. The first time he strikes air. The second time it meets the rough strip on the side of the pack, and the match burns. Without a thought or breath, he drops the match onto the ground, and his body ignites.

The light his engulfed body throws is harsh enough that I have to press myself to the ground to keep safe in the shadows. But still I take pictures of him. It is a once in a lifetime opportunity, after all. Not that I'm showing off. Man set aflame by his own ruined American prosperity. The upper class literally burning itself to ash. It's powerful. People will someday see the images of his death and hear the crackles of his flames, and they will be shocked and moved by the display. And not a single spectator will think of him as a real human being. It's tragedy but only in the Greek sense.

Richard stumbles forward, an inferno on his back and shoulders. He doesn't scream. He doesn't flail or fall. I snap shots of his stoic burning. He marches up the side of the car and reaches toward the rag hanging from the gas tank.

And then that fucking dog.

I don't know if it burrowed or tunneled, if one of the doors were unlocked, but the little white beast of fury comes bounding down the aisle barking madness. Its high-pitched voice breaking the air with every jump it makes toward my encampment. It bolts around my car, and skitters to a stop facing me. About three feet away, it shows its rows of white spikes between black-and-pink gums, and it growls, drool glistens on its chin. It yaps at me, hunches, yaps again, and then lunges. A bolt of white lightning blasting my way as I dash from behind my car. My knees go weak, my legs rubber from staying hunched for so long, and they sway, turning me from where I am trying to aim myself. I stumble and stagger straight into the burning man.

The dog suddenly comes to a stop like it's thrown itself into a wall when it smells the gas, sees the fire, and tastes the smoke in the air. Roger reaches for the rag to set his car into a red-orange-and-white explosion when I fall into him. I knock his arm away before the heat and flame can ignite the rag and blast his girl into a twisted wreck of scorched metal.

His fire in my hair, it jumps and climbs across the arm of my shirt. I am not as strong a man as he is, so I start to scream. I fall to the ground, roll, slap my head and face. I feel the flames flatten to ash under my palms, the heat leaving me. I roll behind some cars. Roger sits slumped against a support column as the passenger side door opens, and that fourteen-year-old blonde brat steps from the vehicle. She sees her dad. A moment passes. I staying lying down, keeping myself pressed to the ground, hidden behind an orange SUV with my jaw cool against the pavement. She doesn't notice me. There's a much larger distraction. She steps toward her burning father. She reaches a hand toward him but still stands feet away. In my prone position I wrestle my camera up to my eye. A gasp hitches in the girl's throat. She screams.

I snap another picture.

Her hand drops, her head falls, her knees give, and she weeps at the feet of his body. I shoot more photos and think of his arm reaching for his car. I saved her. He had meant to murder her, but I stopped him. Not on purpose, but still I'm a hero. A shiver shakes between my shoulders at that thought. I pack my bag and slink away as her rich sobs rise up in pitch, the barking dog running to her. The whole way out of the car park, down the roads, and into the darkness, I look over my shoulder, afraid that she might be following me, begging me to take his place. Don't they say that I'm responsible for her life now? Isn't that what the Chinese believe? I think. But I'm not Chinese, so I'm safe, right?

I think of her tailing me everywhere, expecting me to teach her how to live, how to be.

"Why are you following that person?"

"Do you think you should be taking their picture?"

"This is boring."

"Isn't this illegal?"

"It stinks here. Can't we go home?"

"Are you a psychopath? Are you a creep?"

"I don't think I can love you. You're too weird. You're broken and unnatural."

"Can you take me to mom?"

"Can you get me out of here?"

No, fuck no. She'd cramp my style. I need to be unbound and unburdened to live the lifestyle I choose. Kids change everything.

I duck my head into an arcade and sit at one of the open-air tables outside a sandwich shop that is closed for the night. I look around, but the girl's nowhere to be seen. She never followed me in the first place. I'm safe. Thank god. The responsibility of a girl kneeling at her father's smoldering corpse rolls off my shoulders. She's not my problem. She can be the system's problem. I chuckle to myself, grin at my freedom. That was a close call. I promise myself to never save another girl again.

Jennifer and The Man in Black

When I was a kid, this girl lived at the edge of the block in a half-blown, ramshackle can of a trailer. She was older than me, four-teen or fifteen to my ten. Gossips whispered that she always wore sweat pants and long-sleeved shirts to cover the track marks that ran along her body like black and blue acupuncture points. She had pale lips, dull eyes, ratty hair, and this desolate expression that I'd only ever seen rocks imitate. But those were all things that enchant-ed, enthralled me, the mystery of her, and her unnatural beauty that pulsed from it. However deep I tried to know her, layers of her re-mained masked under her loose clothes and blank stares. The story we told ourselves was that she ran away when she was my age to live with a man six years older than her. Most nights, passing the trailer park, I could hear her yowl like a kicked cat. The sound would stir my skin like the roars of my made-up monsters in the dark.

I wanted to know what a girl like this thought. What a girl like this felt. That's why I followed her when I could. She used to walk past my house every day, just as dusk settled—from work or where, I never knew. There was one night, when my parents weren't home, when I first saw her, and I wondered about her in ways that made it hard to not want to watch her again. I opened the door as she passed the window, and I stepped outside. She looked back, and a tiny spark of shame leaped inside me. But she only scowled, the way she always did.

This is when I learned that she yowled at night, giving me more to wonder about her. Since then I'd see her walking and I'd wonder even more. I didn't stop thinking about her, I couldn't. I needed to know, so that is why I followed her. I would slink after her through the shadows, my head down. Her trailer stood half-slumped only about a quarter of a mile away from my place, but the rush there always held me. My breaths barely slipping from my chest. My palms drawing sweat so quickly that I couldn't stop wiping my palms on my pants. I'd stalked her all the way to the steps of her trailer. I watched her by alone, though her face never seemed to change. I didn't know what I was expecting, but I guess not knowing was part of the excitement.

When once she opened her door, a single light glowed an orange almost brown to her presence, she turned on her porch and looked back into the darkness. "Hey," she called to me. "What are you doing?"

I crouched deeper into the bushes, willing her to have not seen me. I remember my body shaking at being caught, adrenaline racing through my small bones.

She tapped her foot on the metal stairs.

"Come on, I know you're there."

I didn't know what to do, and my legs didn't weren't able to run, so after a brief struggle with myself, I stepped out of the bushes and let her see me for the first time.

"What is it that you want?" she asked.

I shrugged. "To see you," I said, not knowing what it meant, lowering my head in shame.

She frowned, looked past me into the dark behind, then a smirk crossed her lips. It was the first and only different expression I would ever see from her.

"Hey," she called to me again. I looked up, and she lifted her shirt.

Her breasts fell out from under her sweatshirt, large soft slopes with pink nipples. They held my breath frozen in my chest.

I couldn't move. She dropped her shirt just as I was able to commit her with her sweatshirt up over her head to memory.

"Now, get out of here," she said as she turned her back to me and slammed the door.

Those were the first breasts I ever saw. That's how all the following started.

* * *

Two teens make out against a wall behind the club. The boy fumbles with the girl's shirt, lifting it past her stomach, trying to grab a handful of her chest. I crouch in a parking lot across the street, camera zoomed to the action, the microphone crackling with the sounds of their smacking lips. The boy gets her shirt up to the black bra that clasps around her pale curves. I hold steady. He fondles the stiff material, groping through her skin. His fingers wrench the top of her cup and tugs. Her hand snaps around his wrist. She gasps, sighs. She smiles, swallows, and steps back away from him, pushing him off the wall. She straightens her shirt and bra smooth. The boy paces to catch his breath, trying to cool himself. The girl thumbs behind them.

"Let's go back inside," she offers.

"Yeah, right," he coughs.

They head around the side and toward the pounding door of the club.

I lower the camera. Close, but I can't win every night.

Lust is a common theme in my work. Maybe I'll get to say that on a radio show someday. The day people notice. There's something about bodies gnashing in need on streets like this, in the open, something filthy and desperate that everyone needs to see. Maybe it reflects an unrequited desire in myself. All art does, doesn't it?

It's then that I catch something from the corner of my eye. A length of slender shadow enters the parking lot from behind where I've been hiding. I back into a building, its facade throwing darkness over me. The figure paces just at the edge of the parking lot. The body throws looks off in either direction, hair whipping about. I lift the camera to my eye and zoom in for a better look. Black fingernails hold white swirls in the cool air. She's very pretty. She brushes her brown hair back from her face, and I see her. I know her. I know her room number and that grace she held the night my eyes first met her body.

It's Jennifer.

I smirk. Jennifer reminds me of that girl who I followed back to her trailer every night when I was just a boy. She has that same solemnity and mystery trapped in her body. She too enchants me. Maybe tonight Jennifer will catch me, and then maybe she will reveal her bear body to me. All models do, eventually. Layer by layer, stripped down to their essence. It's what they want, even without using words. And Jennifer showing up out of the blue on a night like this right where I can find her, what else could she mean to do? Show me something, my Jennifer. Show me all of yourself.

I run my lens up and down her long but slender slope of a body. I wonder about her breasts. From what I do see I doubt she has much of them hiding under her heavy military jacket. But she could surprise me. I'll only know when I find out. I snap more pictures of her and watch patiently while she waits.

She paces, looking over her shoulder, checking her phone, brushing her fingers through her hair and stamping her foot in the cool evening. She bundles her arms together. It's getting colder out. I can see that she has holes running through her jacket. She also has no hat. I lean back against the cold brick wall wishing that could wrap her arms and her head in mine. I would show her a warm place. We could pull each other close, with her running her fingers over my thighs. She would let me see all of her and keep her soft skin warm.

A man dressed in draping black turns the corner. He nods his head at her; she shifts on her feet, her arms crossed.

"No one's making you stay, you know?" the man tells her. "But no one's making you leave, either. You can keep with us if you want."

Jennifer shakes her head and huffs a breath. "And do what? Be what?"

"Be clean."

She smirks. "Where's the fun? What's supposed to keep me busy?"

"We can keep you busy," the man tells her.

He reaches for her hand, but she pulls away, stepping back a step, before he can touch her. He holds up his hands, understanding.

"We can get you a job. It doesn't have to be with the church. We have so many people working to help you. Why not accept it?"

"Maybe I don't want your help." Jennifer holds her hands like claws.

"Then, don't come looking for it," the man in black tells her. "Because I promise you no one here will offer you anything you don't want."

Jennifer paces a step closer to the priest, holding her head down, pulling her hair away from her ears. "I'm cold, Father."

"Then, come in, at least for the night. If you don't want to stay, then don't stay. No one is holding you against your will."

Jennifer wavers where she stands. She looks the man in the eyes. "Why even keep me a night, if you know you can't save me?"

"Because then I will have saved you for one night."

She wanders toward him, drapes her arms over his shoulders. She presses her face into his chest. Her words are muffled, but the mic pieces them together. "You are too kind for your own good."

The man nods, staring ahead. "That much is true." He pats her back, starts to turn his body. "Come. Let's go back. Let's warm up. In the morning whatever decision you make will be your own."

Jennifer grips a handful of the man's black coat to hold him in place. She looks at him, her eyes widening. "Do you keep me around, just because you like to have me?" she asks.

The priest pauses, holding his words. He pats her hand.

"Let's go."

She stops him again, dragging her feet and gripping his coat.

"You know what would really keep me around, what would really put me in my place, would be a good hearted and strong willed man. That's what I need. That's what will keep me off the streets." She hovers her lips near the priest's chin. "What do you think of that?"

The man in black hold his eyes to the rooftops, where he doesn't look at her. I snap a picture of her body pressing against his like a stripper against her pole. His grimace turned upward toward heaven, and her pout hovering below. It's a beautiful picture.

Jennifer runs a hand down his shoulder. If I were that priest, I would be strong willed. I would be good hearted, if I tried. She lets her lips gently rest on the skin of his neck, and jealousy twists up my guts. But there's nothing I can do. I can't reveal myself. I won't ever see her as she really is, walking to her home at night. I won't ever see her reveal herself fully to me. That only happens if she catches me. But she's not as astute as that girl from my childhood, and I've gotten better at hiding. I thought I loved that girl who flashed me. It's a shame she died.

I swallow back lumps in my throat and click more shots of the two.

The priest holds her shoulder, halting her from rising to her toes to drop her lips onto his.

"I would introduce you to some of the nice men from our congregation, but not until you're well. What you need now is to rely on yourself."

"But I'm broken," Jennifer persists. Her hands travel inside his coat, around his torso, and down toward his pants. The man in black clutches her wrists.

"Why do you try to destroy everyone around you?" he rumbles through his teeth.

"I'm trying to make you realize that there's nothing left to destroy." She places both her palms over his wrist and guides his hand toward her body. "It's all in your head. This whole time you've had nothing to worry about, and you've been wasting yourself behind your made up rules. Maybe I'm here to save you. It's just a different kind of holiness."

The man in black freezes in an open-mouthed mixture of shock and exhilaration. I capture his face in the film. Jennifer guides his hand to the bottom of her jacket. She lifts it as his frozen fingers push past the rim of her shirt and reveals her skin. He grabs at her stomach, then her ribs, and finally she shows him her breasts.

Just like the very first time, I lose my breath deep down in my chest.

Her breasts are small gumdrop slopes with brown nipples, and she's showing them to a man of the cloth in a parking lot instead of to me on the front porch of her greasy boyfriend's trailer, but I still feel the way I did when I was a child. I catch a photo as the priest's hands close over them. Now, her breasts will be mine forever.

She drops her shirt around the priest's wrist, and he pulls his hand back. He wipes his palm on his pants like her nipple could leave a residue.

"You need to calm yourself," he warns her.

"Maybe it's you that needs to calm yourself." Jennifer smirks, looking down on him.

The man in black sighs, holding his composure like a mason at a crumbling wall. He sucks a breath down and lets out a long gust.

"You are not a lost cause," he promises.

"I am a lost cause," Jennifer pushes back. "Otherwise, why don't you lose yourself with me?"

The priest leans back and smacks her across her cheek, and a small shout slips through her lips. She falls sideways without stopping herself, and her shoulder smashes the pavement. She yowls, rolling onto her back. The man in black stares at his hand, turns his palm and examines his knuckles. His eyes pan to Jennifer on the ground, and he opens his mouth, but words won't come. He drops to his knees, resting his hand on her shoulder.

"I'm so very sorry," he whispers. "I'm so—really, I didn't even mean to."

Jennifer looks at him, her eyes fitting to water. She loops an arm behind his neck, so he can help her up, as he lifts her, standing straight up, holding her close. She leans her head in. Their lips touch. His hands squeeze her towards him as she kisses him. Her hand drops under his cloak as he holds her, her fingers stroking at his pants.

"This is what happens when you're so wound up," she whispers into his mouth.

I could be that wound up, I think. I could slap her, if it made her kiss me. I swallow more lumps back and watch her desperately.

She reaches under the band of the priest's pants. He leans his head back, tightening his eyes shut.

"I can't," he pleads.

"I know, not here," she whispers. "But you have a place. Take me there."

I can see that the priest isn't thinking, he only walks, carrying her around the corner and down the street.

My legs tingle with pinpricks from my ankles through my thighs as I try to stand. I stumble, my legs having been crouched for an hour now. I smack them to get the blood rushing, but I don't have the time to straighten myself out with the risk of losing the two of them. I run with my shoulder slumped against the wall to keep steady as my legs fumble their way around the corner.

My headphones crack with the scrape of the microphone dragging against the ground, the wind of it sweeping against the air rustling in my ears. I catch a couple of their words.

"What are you going to do to me?" she asks.

"I don't know." The man says licking his dry lips. "It's been a long time."

"Your first?"

"Not my first."

They turn more corners. The priest paces in a long gait. She rushes besides him playing inside his pants. His breathing runs heavy, cool evening sweat slicks his forehead. My shaking legs weave me across the street, so I can hold pace with them and capture their sin for my eternal memories.

At the foot of the cathedral, with its ship-bottom doors, the man in black sets Jennifer back to her feet. She removes her hand from his pants and licks her fingers. She offers one to the priest. He turns his head, a grimace smearing his face.

"You're definitely ready," she teases.

The priest nods his head and waves a hand in front of himself. Jennifer takes the lead up each step. He unlocks the locks and pulls open one of the double doors, the low red of flickering candle lights sweeps over the walls and weaves through the air behind her.

"Come on, Father. It's time for you to tell me your sins," she says as she taps her fingernails on the door.

The man in black takes a heavy step up the stairs.

"You could not handle all my sins."

"Well that good because I only hope to handle one of them."

He reaches the top of the stairs, where they stare through each other, a mix of war and lust. Then the man in black pulls the door shut behind them. It slams like the gates of hell swinging closed. I stay awhile, snapping pictures of the front of the church, hoping to see some window light up, the shine of Jennifer's face against the stained glass. Maybe I'll get lucky twice tonight and see her naked again, even if it is in the hands of a priest. Maybe then she'll see me. Maybe then she'll want me. I know my logic is weak, but it's all I have. Just a spectator desperate to break onto the stage.

Suddenly the doors swing open. Jennifer holds her face in her hands. Her foot glances off the edge of the top stair, and she loses her balance. She screams as a trio of people chase her through the door, but there's nothing there to stop her fall. She topples head first onto the stone steps. Her back cracks down next, her shoulders striking last, as the side of her head bashes the pavement below. Shamefully she bundles herself up and screams into the ground. Two nuns in their long robes run to Jennifer. They crouch and hold her arms as she sobs. They pull her to her feet, and she looks with running eyes at the priest in the threshold, painted from behind by the candlelight.

"Lying's a sin too you know," she murmurs to him.

"Come back inside," the man in black says.

"It's too cold outside. Come inside and sleep. We can look after your injuries inside. Please, rest yourself. You're not a wild animal. No one, not even you, should have to run and lash and never stop for a moment's peace."

Imaging herself a wild animal, Jennifer bares her teeth at the nuns. She hisses up at the priest. But she lets the nuns hold her under her shoulders and walk her, step by step, up the stairs and back to the front of the church doors. They walk her through, and shut the doors behind her again.

I lower my camera. I could burn the church down for what they just did. If they are so worried about it being too cold outside why not set the building on fire? There are already so many candles inside, one could have just fallen over. A fire like that could burn the whole church down. Then Jennifer could run out. She could see me, and she would recognize me just from the sight of me. We would block the door so that no one else could escape, and she would make love to me on those stairs that so battered her so that she could be healed. The heat of the fire would sizzle the sweat on our skin from the exertion of our bodies pounding together. She would run her hands through my hair and know then that she needed me, and I would do the same. And in the morning we would be found curled together while the church kept us warm with its hot embers, and the skeletons of the priest and his nuns in the smolder. We would wake and kiss and walk through the rubble of the ruins together. And we would be happy.

But I don't have any matches with me, so my dear girl, my captured damsel will have to remain in her tower for another night. Why couldn't she look behind herself one time? Why couldn't she see me? No one ever sees me, even when I'm right behind them in their shadows. Instead she offers herself to another man who doesn't want her, another man who doesn't deserve her.

My stomach twists. Maybe she does see me, and she just doesn't care.

As I leave, I walk past an alley glowing red, and I peek in. A fire bends in a green dumpster, its light dancing against the walls on both sides. A filthy woman with two boys under her arms sleeps against a wall. I stalk to the fire. Her eyes slide open when my shadow spreads over her like a summoned demon's, and though she sees me, she doesn't say a word to me as I peer into the flames. A loose board stands partially out of the fire, and I take hold of it. I pull it free, and the embers I shook loose sweep up overhead. I grin. This is exactly what I need. So, I leave this woman and her children and run back to the church, the burning board in my hand.

I press the flame to the wall on the side of the building. The fire pulls itself apart against the stone and mortar. I run my hobo's torch up and down and across. It throws sparks in all directions, but nothing catches. I then run it along the ground. The fire eats up the board closer to my fist. I can feel the flames sizzling near my skin. I press the fire to one of the double doors, and it starts to sear black, but it doesn't catch before the board burns down to my hand, and the flames eat into my knuckles. I hiss, drop the fire, and kick the plank. I kiss my fist and watch as the fire lowers to nothing against the ground.

Shit.

I turn to face the street again, and three bodies stand at the foot of the steps. The mother, just a couple of years older than me, her brown face marked dark with dirt, stands on the sidewalk holding one of her twin boys under each arm. The three stare at me, all holding empty expressions. With the exception of deep streaks of filth marking their skin, the trio stands naked in front of me. The mother's breasts hang flat, nipples pointing down, her stomach running loose in rolls. My heart skips. My mouth opens, but what words do I have? This isn't the woman who I want to have notice me. There's no mystery to her, no allure. I feel caught and strange, so I jump off the steps and pace with my hands shoved in my pockets and shoulders hovering near my ears, feeling their eyes like spiders on the back of my neck. My body shivers. I decide not to look back.

One of the double doors opens. I hear a voice. "Is there anyone out there?" the man asks.

I risk a glance back. He stands in front of the door, light falling down the stairs and bathing the mother and her two sons in a shallow glow. The man in black moves an arm to them.

"Do you need a place to stay for the night? It's too dark, too cold. Please, come in."

The mother watches him with her blank eyes. She looks to her shivering sons, and she nods. The mongrel family carries their nakedness up the stairs, past the man in black, and into the warm light. The door shuts behind them, and the light closes on me, leaving me in the shadows. I walk through the dark, putting my camera in my bag, feeling caught and guilty, and thinking of that beautiful naked girl on her trailer's porch, wondering if she really did die, and wishing that stalking people was as easy as it used to be.

Frisky

He mounted his mate down the crawl of a dark alley. Both born on the streets and ready to raise hell. She called to him, waved her ass, ensnaring him. He chased her down, and has his back arched while she howled and struggled under him, turning her head to lash at him, drawing blood, fighting but losing. The black beast didn't care. He held stiff inside her as he shuddered and grumbled, digging in deep and letting loose.

I called him Frisky. He looked like a Frisky to me. Though I've never been good at naming animals.

He finished, twisting off of her body and leaping over a dumpster to escape his lover's slashing claws. Love is just as much about avoiding as much bloodshed as possible.

It reminds me of my first time. Not by much, but just enough. Everyone remembers their first. An unlucky few, like me, can remember each time after as well. There have only been a few blips on my radar of willing women. Maggie was one. She caught me in an alley like this. It was on one of my late night trips, before I knew the streets well enough to find a way to the place I would call home. I was sitting alone in that alley, thirteen years old, quaking, the streetlights shattered and dark, while a pair of large men made devious eyes at me. Dangerous stares like those that my dad would fire at me so that I knew their subtle details.

The girl was filthy. A pot-marked face, but with a cheery enough smile. Cheerful against the surroundings, anyway. Her auburn hair covered one of her eyes and curled down her shoulders. She pushed it back to see. Her small nose had freckles. She was fifteen to my thirteen, two full years my senior.

I shot photographs as I chased the cat I called Frisky weaving and winding over the higher points of the city. In the shadows, he stalked like a pint-sized panther, jet black fur crouched, and yellow eyes scanning for another fuck or a kill. I had to shoot him with a flash, so that his dark shape would stand out against the cityscape. He hissed at my light, yowled, and leapt away. I dashed to keep pace with him, twisting around a corner just to see him leap a fence. I broke down the next alley and find him again, skulking across the street. The way he moves, blends into the shadows, the way he hates being seen, hates being noticed, reminds me of myself.

Plus I have been known to be frisky too.

Maggie crawled in a basement through a broken window. She guided me in, pressing her finger to her lips. She made a small fire out of broken furniture legs and balled up magazines. We had to keep the flames away from the window, so no one would see the, the black smoke from the burning glossy papers clogging our lungs. We tried to find the right place to sit where we were close enough to the fire to warm ourselves without suffocating. She told me her mom and dad were killed by a drifter. He had let himself into their house, skewered her parents with the half-moon pull-hoe they kept in the garage, and kidnapped her. She said she spent weeks with him in an empty house just blocks away, before she was able to chew through the rope that held her to the radiator and run away. She didn't go to the police, because then he would find her, and he would get her. He had promised her he would, and so she didn't give him the chance.

"But it's very lonely down here," she told me as we laid side-by-side beneath the slick smoke. Somebody rumbled and moved upstairs. I stiffened. She patted my hand and assured me that those people never came down here.

Frisky was more than a sex maniac, it would seem. He was a psychopath, if a cat can be such a thing, with a need for spilled blood and broken bones. The animal instincts that keep his eyes sharp and his senses honed all tune him for murder, making him a fierce king in his world. He dove from a fence post, slamming his claw over the head of a desperate rat. It shrieked, and writhed. Frisky held the little animal under his fist. Blood bubbled from its head, trickling onto the concrete, wetting it like the rains. I flashed a shot of the murderer, holding his prey's head down, and the cat didn't shy that time. He didn't run. He was engrossed with his kill. I flashed another shot, and the cat looked straight at me. Like he knew. Like he approved of my taking his picture.

Maggie's the one who took off her clothes first. She told me that she almost never wears them down there anyway. They always stink, and they were so dirty that they itch. But they were all that she had. She only got dressed to go outside when she had to find food, otherwise she'd be naked always. She laid down next to me. I was breathing hard, and not just because of the black smoke twisting down my throat, but because she was well formed and fully visible in the flickering firelight. She rolled to her side, touched my face, and asked if I wanted to see some of the things the drifter taught her.

I did.

Frisky bounded up the fire escape still clutching his half-dead rat in between his teeth. The creature twisted and moaned. I turned on my mic and lifted it toward the climbing cat and his snack. It was too late for much noise to cross the roads, so the clink of the fire escape, the growl of the cat over his kill, and the struggles of the almost dead thing in his teeth sounded straight into my recording.

Frisky reached a landing near the top floor. I could barely see his small body for the metal, brick, and shadows of the building. But I caught the flick of his tail and the battering of the rat's. Frisky turned his head to look over the edge of the escape, and he opened his jaws. The rat fell, plummeting, twisting over itself, straight to the ground, where it cracked with the sound of a spitball hitting just behind your ear. Its leg kicked once before it went still.

A devious bastard of a cat.

I crossed to the kill and lifted my camera. It batted its tail, lying in a mangled shape of jagged bones and crooked muscles. Its nose faced its tail, and its arms pressed into its chest. Blood swelled around it, glistening in the flash of my shot, filling the background. I looked up the building again. Frisky leapt down one floor at a time and reached the ground next to me. He strutted off, waving his tail, and leaving the rat behind. At the corner of the road, he looked back at me. I followed.

I was never to have sex like the first time I had sex. I didn't even really understand the finer points of masturbation with no one to show it to me. I had tried and finished a few times, but I never really got the art of it. And then she climbed on top of me, her face disappearing into the thick smoke. Not that it mattered since I had closed my eyes. She didn't make any noise. She didn't have to. She was able to work her insides like I've never felt someone do since. She flexed and held my cock tight when she slowly slid up and then let go to pound down onto my hip bones with her soft ass checks. As she rode me up and down, she captured a rhythm, like a song you could only feel, making my ears ring. I quickly finished once, too quickly for her, so she kept at it, until I finished again. Then and only then did she fall next to me, running her fingernail down my chest.

She started to carry.

Frisky found another female feline to fuck, and she cried out in more powerful screams than the other lady cat had.

Dull sobs dropped from Maggie that night.

I flashed more shots, but he didn't care. He lived for it. He looked at me, with eyes that say, 'are you getting all this?' I was; I got every pump.

When he finished, this female attacked him too. She slashed the blood from his chest and another long gash under his eye. He ran like a caught kid and twisted into the dark. I thought that I might lose him after that, but he showed up under a street light a block away, sitting with his tail curled under him, waiting, watching, like he knew that there was more to show me, like I was of some use to him. Once I caught up, he led the way.

A true entertainer, this one.

Maggie cried as she held me close, the smoldering flames of the furniture fire dwindling. I didn't know what to do. I remember my head spinning. I didn't understand why she had cried when it had felt so good. So I closed my arms around her and pressed my chin against her shoulder, and I let her cry it all out on me. She wept and shuddered in my arms, and I didn't know that it was possible to feel so wanted. Finally she pulled her head back, and our eyes met for the first time. She leaned forward, our lips meeting as well. That was my first kiss. It was all a little in reverse but still meaningful.

By then the pounding upstairs had grown into a rumble as it reached the door that sloped down to our basement. And then that door opened.

Frisky lurked back roads, and I tried to follow at a similar canter, matching the way he lowers himself, the smoothness of his movements. I knew I couldn't match them with my angles and bone structure, but I tried. I wished I could be a cat, to disappear into and own this city, not to just be a part of it. I was a light post, and him a bullet train.

The rumble and growl of the dogs struck the mic and shook into my headphones. Frisky froze mid strut and stiffened. His hair perched to spikes up his back and along his neck. He hissed at the air. He looked over at me, and I shook my head towards him, but he already knew what he wants to do. He's not the king. These dogs were kings, and he had plans to overtake that throne.

The dogs prowled in packs along the streets at night. The pack that Frisky tracked totals six, all mutts with mangled faces and broken noses. They barked, howled and jumped at each other, drilling claws and teeth into each other's necks and sides. Once they caught sight of me, they kept their distance. Enough beatings have taught them to fear me based on my shape. I hung back allowing Frisky to take his chance. He strutted along a fence where the dogs were tearing into the guts of a dead raccoon, killed by a car. They smacked their jaws and slapped at each other's faces to get into the stomach of the road kill, some whimpering, others growling, none satisfied.

Frisky peered over the ledge of the fence at his prey. He looked up at me, crouched across the street with my Canon to my eye. He seemed to nod at me saying 'got this?' before diving down.

The feet came pounding down the stairs. Maggie was too busy holding me and shaking and sobbing to hear them, and I was too weak and drained to push her off quickly enough. A round man in suspenders was shouting hell when I went for the window, crawling through. Maggie screamed. Then the old woman called down the stairs, but I could make no words through the cacophony. Maggie tried reaching for me, but I had already jumped up and was pulled myself through the window hole. I turned on my chest and looked back down into the basement. The man had grabbed Maggie by the hair. She struggled, shrieked as he called for the woman upstairs to call the police. Maggie lashed her hands toward me, staring at me with wild eyes that broke open with tears of terror. My stomach tied itself into a knot, my heart freezing on a beat, My lungs stopping. I lowered my eyes, as the man dragged Maggie by her hair away from the window and toward the stairs.

Frisky threw me those same eyes when as he dug his claws into the face of a dog that yelped and shook him lose. The pack broke into a fury, throwing their teeth and legs toward the intruder. A pair of jaws latched around him and closed down on him. The dog holding Frisky in his fangs lifted his head around the others who sat back, watching, hoping for their own piece. Frisky screeches turned my headphones into crack static. He lashed toward me; throwing me his eyes, but I stayed put. I've always stay put. His stomach burst open, the dogs shouting and leaping in victory. The dog holding Frisky got knocked aside by the others, and the corpse of that cat fell to the ground. They bent and snarled and tore him to pieces with their murdering mouths, and all I could do is snap pictures.

I ran from Maggie's basement. Naked, pumping my arms besides me, into the dark. I held back my fear and tears and a complete lack of understanding of what had just happened, until I reached a familiar alley where I could fall into a corner and crumple and cry. Why had she been so nice to me? Why did she cry afterwards? Why did they take her? Why had they been so mean? Why didn't I save her? I stared at my own knuckles trembling on the sidewalk. I closed my eyes against the dark, thinking of Maggie's face, whispering, "I'm sorry."

I couldn't be anything like Frisky.

I can't be a king. I can't fuck who or what I want. I can't kill what I want. I won't take risks. I don't own the city. The city owns me. I only follow and run. I never lead. I find what's left of his ribs and skull on the ground after the dogs have parted. I run a finger down his body. A tear strikes his head. I pull him close to my chest, cradle him in my arms as tears run my face.

"I'm sorry," I whisper to my dead friend and my stolen lover. "I'm sorry. I'm sorry." I'll always be sorry.

I shoot pictures of his guts and viscera, hoping that someday his sacrifice will have been for something.

Leon

Skin crafted by Tom Ford, a Bowflex body, and hair held in place with the oil from dozens of clubbed baby seals. A real man's man. He smiles and laughs easily, showing big white teeth that can crush bone, a square jaw that can break brick. He draws all the attention, sucking it in like a black hole and holds it deep in his chiseled chest. In a movie about his life, he'd play himself.

And in the camera of my eye, he's playing the role he was born for. The American ideal. My ideal.

I call him Leon. He drinks alone, surrounded by strangers, no one saying his name. I sit closer to him than I usually do to this man. And though I haven't touched him yet, he's real. Real as plastic or stone. Unblemished and waiting to receive the life the only I can give him.

I wish I could touch him.

"Africa," he recounts to any soul sitting at that bar. "Little boys, filthy, covered in sores, flies everywhere, like I'd never seen before. When I came upon them, they were drowning in a pool of mud, fallen into a sudden sinkhole that had opened below them, , their heads barely above the filthy water, their arms flailing, eyes terrified, sinking fast. My guide warned me to leave them. Because of the diseases, the parasites that would be floating in that water. But I didn't worry about it. I didn't even think about it. I just acted. Because that's what you do when people are in trouble.

Two little boys for the life of one man? Seemed like a fair bargain. Who of you would think twice, really? I dove in. I didn't breath; I didn't swallow. I did keep my eyes open. By then the boys were lost, they were so far under, the water so brown, that I could bare- ly make out their lashing arms. I dived deeper, foot after foot, until I finally saw something kicking. Then, I saw the other. I grabbed each of their spindly arms in one fist and kicked off the bottom of the pit, shoving myself to the surface. I dragged them over the edge and onto the ground, pulling myself up. My guide told me I was down there, in the sink hole, for at least ten min- utes, underwater. But I didn't feel that. They say that the need to save someone gives people superhuman abilities. Well, I think that's true. I am living proof of that. And those boys are, too."

The crowd murmured. Women touch his back and arms. He grins and drinks. People throw more money on the counter to keep him drinking and to keep him talking, like a trained mon- key dancing for coins. I wait to follow him, wait until everyone is more drunk on booze than they are on him, wait until they give him the opportunity to escape with the finest of the women he can rustle from this dive.

He doesn't leave with the ones he chooses until three. He's been drinking all night—whiskey, rum, beer, vodka, whatever they'd serve him—but it doesn't show. His gait is measured and smooth. Two women hold him by his arms. As he gets to the door he stops, breathes the night through his nose. "We won't need to walk," he tells his women. "We can ride home in style."

Shit. I've tried to follow cars before, and I either lose them if I let them get too far or nearly get hit by them if I get too close. I'd like to do neither tonight.

Leon takes his cell phone from the Valentino jeans he wears and calls for a car. His voice smooth and cool. the kind of voice that runs with charisma and suavity. He chats easily with the women as they wait under a streetlight.

I stand at the far end of the street watching from the corner. Enough couples and lonely drunks wander the sidewalk between us that I feel comfortable here so in the open. Not that anyone would notice the suspicious guy watching the guy that everyone else is watching. He's an easy target. But if he gets in a car and speeds off, then I will have to find someone less interesting to follow, someone less fulfilling. I don't want to waste the night when such a special specimen of a man stands before me.

I imagine myself getting close to him, maybe gaining his friendship. We'd sit at a table together, him next to me, maybe our arms even touching, crowds forming around us. I'd be interesting by my association, maybe wanted by the women who couldn't have him. I'd be their second best. That would be exciting. I've never been anyone's second best. He'd tell me his secrets, secrets about himself that he'd never have told anyone else. He'd train me in the art of him, tutor me in his ways. And in time, with his help, I'd become him. Maybe then I'd have to kill him, to become number one. I know I could do it, if I felt that I was strong enough, skilled enough, that I could replace him. What man wouldn't? Certainly not me.

The car pulls up, it's a black cab. And suddenly I have a bad idea, but, I think to myself, a bad idea is better than no idea at all, so I go for it. I run towards them, and I throw myself into the pavement curb at their feet. First my shoulder cracks the concrete, then my skull. I roll over on the ground below them. I hold my head with one hand, my knee with the other. I hiss and grunt pain at Leon's feet. He looks down on me, as he should, his women looking at him, not knowing what to do.

"Shit," I hiss lying there. "Someone tried to mug me. I was running to get away. I think I twisted my ankle."

Leon steps forward; his women at his back. "It's all right." He says leaning in, and then he touches me. Adonis touches my skin, and I feel his power radiate into me. I wonder if he sees something of that in my expression, because he grimaces when we match eyes. But his face falls to its natural heroic grace in a moment. He holds me by my back and my stomach and helps me to my feet. "Did this robber chase you?"

"I'm not sure." I look over my shoulder, panting. "Maybe. I hope not."

"Where are you headed?"

"I just need to get out of this place, it's not safe."

He nods, looks at his women, then pats my shoulder. "Get in my car."

His fist of justice opens the back door for me, and I slide in across the black leather interior. The inside of the car is black on black on black, like sitting inside the night itself. Leon has to talk his women into entering the car, now. They look at me and hold their painted lips in frowns. He speaks, moves his hands, persuades and seduces. I can't hear what he's saying, and it'd be rude to pull out my equipment, now, so I just guess.

Leon opens his arms. "Ladies, if you want me, you'll have to get in the car with this one little disgusting man. Just for a short ride."

One woman looks at her friend and grimaces words. "We don't have to touch him, do we?"

He holds her shoulder and leans in close to mouth reassurance. "Of course not. I wouldn't want you making your hands filthy on him before you have a chance to rub my unblemished skin." He holds her hands. "The things these fingers will feel. And all you have to do is get in the car."

The other girl jabs a finger straight at me and mouths four words, "He might kill us."

Leon holds her hand, running his teeth in a curt phrase. "I'd kill him first."

They seem calmed by this—shoulders lower, faces straighten. They breathe, and he leads them into the car. He slides in next to me, a divider between the beautiful women and the scum-streaked sort-of-a-man that I am.

Leon tells the driver where they're going, and the figure at the wheel drives. Most of the ride is silence, the women throwing pained expressions my way, Leon unsure how to ease the situation.

"So, you were mugged?" Leon asks me.

"Almost."

"Must have been terrifying. I've never been mugged, or attacked, or anything of the sort. I can't imagine how that would feel. I'm sorry."

I can't help but smile a little. He's showing me sympathy. He's talking to me instead of these beautiful women who want him. Maybe he pities me a whole hell of a lot for not being him. Maybe he'll take me under his wing. Maybe the time will come that I do kill him and take his place. And why not? He's not a real person, only as real as my pictures make him to be. I would like very much to his place, I think. Maybe that's why we've been pulled together. I shrug at him.

"It all happened so fast. He had a gun—and a knife."

"My god," he says.

"Yeah, a gun and a knife," I say as I look out the window.

"I think he even fired a shot after me. I didn't even have much of anything for him to take. Some people are just so low down. Especially compared to you, I would guess."

"Don't say that," Leon says griping my shoulder, turning my eyes to his. He holds my gaze with steady steel.

"Every man is the same. Fortune, fame, strength, and looks are nothing, if a man isn't the person he wants to be. That's all there is. Just be who you want to be, and the rest will follow."

"Thanks," I nod.

He's already teaching me his secrets, and he doesn't even know it.

The black car stops outside an apartment building. It's not a bad place, but it's not the glitz and glamour I was expecting from him. It's brick, tall. I'm sure he lives on the top floor and has a delightful story for why he chose such a quaint place. There's no fence around it, no guards, nothing that I'd expect from a man like him.

As he prepares to get out, he adjusts in his seat, reaching into his back pocket, and pulls out a silver wallet indented with snakeskin ridges. He flips it open and removes a black card with the word Platinum etched on it. Leon hands this card to the driver, and the driver swipes and returns it without looking back at us. Leon closes his wallet, sits on all that cash again. He waves to his ladies. "Let's go." Then, he looks back at me. "Have the car take you wherever you want. Don't worry about paying, I've got this. I'm sorry that you had such a stressful night."

At first cold confusion hits me. Then, a pang. He doesn't want me with him. I won't be his number two. He doesn't need one. I swallow the disappointment piling up in my throat. "Thank you," I whisper.

The door opens. He nods to me, and he and his women exit the car.

"Where to?" the driver asks, not looking back.

I watch out the window a while longer, staring as the elite strut to their front door. Leon frees a new card from his wallet. He stops a moment to talk to the women.

"Shit," I mutter, fishing into my bag.

"Where to?" the driver asks again.

I pull out my camera, assemble it. I lift it to my eyes, and my sight tightens, focuses, and clears. Leon lifts his arm and sets it around one of the girl's shoulder. The face of the card shows clearly under the floodlight of the building. I snap a shot and breathe easy as Leon swipes the card, and the three enter, pacing over a red-carpet interior like fucking movie stars.

"Excuse me," the driver says raising his voice. "Where do you need to go?"

"Here's fine," I say and push the door open. I try to walk normally, pacing down the street from the apartment building, waiting. As soon as the car's engine growls, and it rumbles down the street and away, I turn on my heel and stalk back to the base of the building. I slink in the shadows along the grass, away from the light. It's twenty stories or more. I hunker near the side wall and look at my camera. I find the last photo I shot and read the golden number on Leon's cream colored card. 22 – P. The twenty-second floor, room P. Shit, that'll be some work.

His fire escape hovers out of reach, but I have my tools. I unzip my bag, and inside is a metal hook at the end of a rope. I remove and swing it upward. The hook snags the bottom rung. I pull dropping the ladder. I climb in, then I pull the ladder up behind me, leaving no trace of myself on the ground.

The black metal staircase creaks and sways as I climb up slowly on all fours. I keep close to the scaffold out of fear of toppling off and falling to my death. Even from the second story my bones would break and probably couldn't be mended. Ten times that height, and what would be left of me? Not that the death of a stalking creep trying to scale an apartment building would be a great loss, but it would still be a loss.

I reach the seventh floor, the ground blurring below me, when I wonder how often fire escapes are serviced. My guessed answer doesn't bring much solace, but I continue to climb. At times like these I do wonder what's wrong with me, but not enough to stop.

At the fifteenth floor, the metal shudders, and something snaps. Luckily the fire escape doesn't lurch or start to fall, but I wonder how many bolts can snap before the whole steel trap collapses? I look to the city skyline, which, terrifies me. I strain my eyes to the wall and hold my breath. I am brick. I am steel. I won't fall. I'll have to climb back down this escape when I leave, my stomach twisting itself into a knot of acid.

The twenty-second floor is one from the top. On the landing there's a single metal door—locked—and a window. I peer through the glass, into the dark. A thin line of grey light seeps through the room behind the window. The outline of a sink, a refrigerator glow in the dark. There is a table, it's clean, no silverware, no plates, nothing to attract insects or displeasure. The man doesn't disappoints. He really is the one. The one that God men say don't exist, so they don't have to feel insecure or inadequate, praying to their dead instead. But they should, everyone should. I know I do. Feel insecure, that is.

I pull at the window, but it's locked. I press my back to the wall and catch my breath, a feeling vacuuming the air from my stomach. I close my eyes and try to forget the height, as the wind blows, and the escape sways and groans. I was to tear my skin from my bones, if it means getting away safely. I can't breathe. I need off of here. So, I do something stupid instead. I grab my bag, and slam it through the window, shattering the glass. It isn't quiet or reserved, but I'm not feeling those ways either. I crawl myself through the opening without waiting to see if anyone comes. I huddle against my bag on the floor, kicking myself under the kitchen table, and I wait, knowing that this was a mistake that I can't escape.

But no footsteps chase me in; no voices call out. The lights don't shoot on. No one catches me. A steady hiss of a shower running sounds somewhere in the other rooms. I slide out from under the table, slow my breath, and calm myself.

I take in his kitchen. His silverware is actually silver. Every knife, even the butter knives are sharp as they glisten. His plates are china, his glasses immaculate. He has a large collection of wine glasses, tumblers, and shot glasses. The food he keeps is all fresh, vegetables, fruits—most of which I don't know the names for. They sit without names in his cool crisper and in bowls on the counter. His meats are red enough that if I broke the seal, the slabs would squeal. I sniff the inside of his fridge. There is no lingering odor of spills or messes left unattended. It's clean enough to be for show. But it's not. This man is real, and the only camera on in this apartment is the one I carry hooked under my arm.

His living room is just as immaculate. A black rug and a black coffee table. A black and chrome fireplace mounted under a sixty inch TV. A black love seat, two black chairs. I snap a picture of the furniture. I feel like a photographer for a home decor catalog. Up the hallway minimalist art hangs over one door, the door to the bedroom of bedrooms, his master bedroom. It is closed. I lower myself to my hands and knees, and I peer under the doorway. Two pairs of pale feet tap the floor—hardwood. Voices murmur, the two women talk softly to themselves. The hissing in the shower stops, and the two bodies shift, their feet following. A door opens, and I can smell the steam.

Leon's heavy feet enter my thin frame.

"Make yourselves as at home as you like," he says. "This isn't a church."

"We heard something in the kitchen," one woman's voice starts.

The moment's silence weighs down my chest as I hold my breath, my heart hammering against my eardrums.

The other woman picks up. "Something shattered. We didn't want to go looking without you."

"Okay," Leon's feet already turning toward the door. Quickly, I straighten up, and slink down the hallway. I slip into the dark living room and crouch behind the couch against the wall. I try to calm myself. Even if they find me, they won't hurt me. I can hurt them instead. I can run away. I can escape down the fire escape. No matter what happens I can get out of here.

Unless they do hurt me, or hold me here, in which case I may end up in jail. I'm not sure how many laws I've broken or how many they'd learn I've already broken from searching the contents of my bag. Too many to count for right now, I'm sure.

Just as I'm tucking myself in, the door opens, and light cascades in a bar down the hallway and into the kitchen. I'm paint. I'm plaster. I'm wallpaper. Leon marches down the hallway and turns towards the kitchen. His back faces me, glistening with water, a thick black towel wrapped around his waist. He flips on the kitchen light. The room glows, and he sees the fragments of glass hanging in the window and littering the floor. "Huh," he grunts. The two women follow behind him into the kitchen. They cluster around the window. Leon taps his chin. "How in the hell did something like this happen?"

"Did someone just break in?" one girl asks.

Leon huffs, "Twenty-two floors up seems doubtful. No one's ever broken in before." He leans his head out the window, looks around, pulls it back in. "Maybe a bird crashed into it? Do you girls want a drink?"

"Absolutely," one says.

I take my chance while their backs face me, slip out from behind the couch, turn into the hallway, and creep along the floor into the master bedroom.

And there is where the king slumbers. The bed is a California King. A long red blanket falls over it with matching pillows and matching curtains behind it. Curtains thin enough to let the sun billow through in the morning and the moon and stars shine at night. On the nightstand, his wallet sits. Smooth snakeskin, fat with cards. His keycard to. If I take it, I won't have to take the death stairs down now, if I don't want to.

A thin line of steam still trails from his bathroom. I smell the heat, and follow it. What does a man who stands above all other men wash himself with? Soaps with French names. I open my bag and shove a few inside. What sort of pills does he take? I open his medicine cabinet and find colognes and make ups. I drop them in my bag. Prescription pills I can't pronounce the names of. I wonder if he needs them or if they're for fun. What a dumb question. Like this man needs any medication. I drop them in my bag. He uses a straight edge like a barber. He has his own grooming kit and a professional blow dryer. There's drain cleaner under the sink. Silently I zip up my bag and stalk back into the bedroom again. I snap a photo of it, of the view of the city, black with squares of lights shining in far-off buildings. Then I slink back into the living room.

In the kitchen, the three drink and chat. One woman teeters in her chair and stands. She struts and peers out the broken window. "I want to go out there," she says in a loud voice that wavers. "I want the air. Maybe there's something to see out there."

"Come on, stay in here," Leon says as he stands. "That's not funny. You could hurt yourself on the glass."

He holds her hips, and she laughs, slaps his wrists away. "I'll be fine. You might not know it from looking at me now, but I was a decent tomboy when I was a kid. I'd climb trees higher than any of my brothers. I wanted to play football, but girls can't. Isn't that dumb? Why not? Boys used to call me a lesbian."

"Stay inside," Leon continues.

"I just want to see what it's like out there. I'm not gonna fall."

Leon starts another protest, but she's already unlocking the door and pushing herself through the broken glass. She laughs drunk, falling onto the landing. She shouts into the kitchen where the other woman sits and nurses a tumbler of gold and Leon stands watching. "Oh, come out. It's cold out here! The metal is so cold! If anyone's climbed up here, they must be freezing."

Funny, I didn't even think about the cold what with all my fear.

The woman's figure shows black as a shadow against the sky dark blue, the sun just starting to rise in a sliver of gold. She holds herself on the railing, looking out. "Oh, wow. This is cool. Wow. The sun is really cool."

"Great, you've seen it," Leon starts. "Now, please come inside. It's not safe."

"Don't you ever wish you could grab the stars?" she shouts back. "Sometimes I wish." And she leans forward, reaching out, as the fire escape screeches. The metal twists, the landing lurches, and the woman shrieks. Her silhouette disappears from the window. Leon rushes, reaches out. The other woman stands, knocks her chair back. She clasps her hands over her face. It's the best distraction I'll have, and I move for the front door between the living room and kitchen. I unlock it, open it, and slip out, the door automatically locking behind me.

In the landing, I stand, straighten myself. I smooth my shirt. Outside Leon's penthouse is a little marble area with a single elevator door. No stairs. I slip the card through its receiver, and a green light blips. The doors open, and I step through. They close. I press G. The elevator hums and moves as smooth as if it weren't moving at all straight down the building. In less than a minute I reach the ground floor. The doors open. At this hour, the marble lobby stretches empty. No one at the desk, no one at the door. I cross through, hearing the click of my shoes on the floor. The red carpet entrance dampens my footfalls, the front door shutting and locking itself behind me. I smell the cool air and see the street again. I turn and face the building, thinking of swiping my new card, taking the elevator back up, and entering my apartment where my women wait. Instead I exhale. I feel more like Leon than ever before. I wonder if he feels less like himself, now that I've taken pieces of him and carried them off. A bag of the perfect man hangs off my shoulder. A rush pumps into my heart. This was a good night.

As I walk down the sidewalk, past the corner of the building I had climbed, the shine of a curl of blonde hair catches my eye from the grass in the lot next door. I stop. The curl connects to the scalp of a head. Face down, her head had exploded, her stomach too with guts that reek of bile. Lying there, she has no legs; they're in the bushes. Her arms shot off, one gripping the grass in the dawn farther down the side of the building, and the other in the street clawing at the sidewalk. Streaks of blood trace their trajectory. I stare up the building so far that my neck aches, and I see angles. I find the top floor. The fire escape hangs from the side. Like a pro, I pull my camera out and zoom up. A figure, only his back shining from the light inside the penthouse, hangs half out of the building. Leon, still holding his open hand toward the fire escape, desperately grimaces, pulling his lips, and showing his teeth, his eyes quaking. I snap a picture, then another and another. I can see that he's not feeling like himself tonight. The cracks in our ideals, the imperfections of the perfect. One day some old woman sipping a mint Julip will tell me she found the image striking, that it rattled her deeply. And I'll agree. Neither of us will consider the girl exploded at my feet. That's the power of good art.

I retire my Canon to its bag and trot down the road, my posture straightening, my gait gaining a dancing quality as if I'm walking to a private song in my head. I'd whistle it, but I never learned how. Maybe Leon was right. Maybe it's not the money or the looks or the strength. Maybe it's all in how a man sees himself that makes him the kind of man he is. A good man is a strong man, and a bad man is a weak man. The only perfect people are the ones who can see themselves as who they are. I walk on. Tomorrow I might not believe this, but this morning I do. Today, I feel like the world is mine. I feel like I've stolen fire from a nameless God who I only know as Leon. Maybe it's just a spark, but it's enough to keep me warm.

Today I feel just a little bit away from perfect.

Jennifer?

Sometimes you'll see a crowd of people, and just a flash of hair or the shape of a blurred face turned sideways will make you see someone you think you know. If given enough pieces of different people pressed together in a tight space, you can piece them together into whomever you want.

This happens to me. In the dark, with booze making my brain roll over itself, I sometimes see someone. In a group of young women, all in leather skirts, sandals, and blowing blouses, slapping their way down the sidewalk, laughing and pointing around them, speaking too fast and in tones that only they can understand. I have seen them, they draw attention, like a set of girls who thrive on attention.

In the center of the group, I catch the movement of a hand, the flash and sheen of a black fingernail. I think I know that pale skin, those bones that roll under the knuckles. I follow the group, because that's what I do, and I keep my distance. Other men watch too, from across the street, from inside their cars idling at stoplights. Men waiting to be heroes, to be knights, to tackle the first creep who comes too near these delicate flower bouquets, and to accept their many blowjobs, and open thighs, as reward.

Aware of the others, I sink in the dark, pretending to look at my shoes, sway as if I were more drunk than I am. I stop at street corners and look around as if I don't know which direction to go in. I'm not sure if any of this is necessary. But it sure beats a beating.

Brown hair waves in this group's center. It holds on a pair of tight shoulders, high and boney. I squint, step a pace closer to make her out. Her face turns, flashing ruby lips and a smile as white and luxurious as the ivory of elephant tusks. My mouth opens to say her name, even if it's not really her name. It's the only name I've ever known her by.

Jennifer, I call her.

They cluster outside a club where the music bangs against the walls and the neon floods from within. They huddle, plan, and prepare. A black girl steps from the group. She shakes her head no, lifting a hand to the group. Jennifer steps beside her, her hair and legs long in stride. The rest of the girls get their wrists wrapped and are readied for entrance.

Instead, Jennifer and the black girl walk across the street and around the corner. The thunder of the club dies beyond them, and the number of people along the road thins. They talk over the clap of their sandals on the pavement. The black girl covers her mouth and lays a soft punch on Jennifer's shoulder. She grips Jennifer's forearm tight and pulls her around the corner into an alley with a laugh that smothers itself between the tight brick walls.

I hold my camera against my chest, stalking to the corner. Their shadows stretch across the pavement and into the street, blown out by the streetlights on the other end. I snap photos. The springy hair of the black girl and Jennifer's long hair set their silhouettes apart.

The girl slides her hand onto Jennifer's shoulder. They talk in whispers with words that slither like hissing snakes into the streets, words I couldn't make sense of. One head leans forward, and then the two converge. The black crescents of their shadows become a sphere in the night. I snap a photo of the two of them, and my heart sinks. First her brother, then a priest, now this girl. Every night Jennifer takes someone new, but never me.

I crush my back into the edge of the wall, as I close my eyes a moment, holding my breath. I am concrete; I am paint; I am not a man. I peek past the corner.

The black girl runs her hands down Jennifer's straight hair, to her thighs, where she grips them in her long fingers, running her hands around to the back, and sliding them up to hold her ass. They kiss as she does this. Their lips smack. Their faces changing directions, their lips smacking again. The black girl bubbles up a drunken giggle. She leans forward, holding her head on Jennifer's shoulder, pressing her palms to the wall. She looks up and smiles. They kiss again.

Now, the girl's hand slides up Jennifer's skirt. Jennifer, looking to the sky, lets a quick gasp cut her throat, letting out a shuddering breath, bringing her eyes back down the building to match her lover's.

"Do you like it out here?" the girl asks, holding her eager smile. "Someone could see us," she giggles. At that she leans in and kisses Jennifer before she can respond. I snap another photo. The girl grips a handful of Jennifer's hair with one hand while the other works its way below her skirt. Jennifer closes her eyes; bliss perking her cheeks into a smile.

After their lips part, and Jennifer lets a low sigh slip her lips. The girl pets her, watching her eyes and lips. "You're so hot," she whispers. "You know that?"

Their mouths close again while the black girl, her fingers licked, works her under the skirt again. Jennifer locks her arms around the girl's back, holding her close, inhaling each other's air. A rage twists in me with each click of my Canon, watching Jennifer wrap the ringlets of the other girl's hair around her middle finger. Jennifer's head turns as the black girl kisses her cheek and neck. Jennifer's eyes open, turn and fall on me.

My heart flattens.

Their lips smack together, the saliva-streaked skin parting, but Jennifer holds me in her gaze. She watches me and waits. Me.

She arches her back against the other girl's hand; letting a moan slip her lips, all the while watching me. I lift my camera, snap another picture, which only makes her moan louder. I snap two, three, four, and with each snap her moans rise up to break the sky like the cries of scattering birds.

The girl clasps a hand over Jennifer's face. "Be careful," she whispers and half laughs. "It's not getting caught if we're making sure people know we're here."

Jennifer, ensnaring me with her stare, lifts an arm in my direction. A shiver wracks my spine. She's about to point me out; they'll get the police; I'll be beaten as a pervert and left in the street, bleeding. But she doesn't point to me. She curls a finger towards me, beckoning. Her open lips mouth the words, "Come catch me."

And so I do.

Like wallpaper peeling I step from the corner, standing in the full light of the alley. The new position does not suit the contours of my body well, and I'm sure it shows in the bend of my knees, the hunch of my shoulders, and the slack jaw look I hold when the black girl turns her head to me.

Her eyes widen. She pulls a glistening hand from inside Jennifer and raises it to wave toward me. "Hey, dude," she starts, her voice shivering. "You been there a while? You lost?" She glances back at Jennifer and whispers, "Let's go."

So, I run after them. I can't lose Jennifer this time. Not again. I didn't go into that motel room; I didn't burn that church to the ground. What if this is my last chance? What if this is the moment where I either make myself known or I lose her forever? Some people may not want a girl who spends as much time on the streets as I do, keeping sordid company, but maybe that's why she fits me so well. That's why she needs me. That's why she called to me.

I catch the black girl by the elbow and pull her back. She yells. I throw her against the wall and take Jennifer's wrist. "We can go," I tell her. The first words I've ever said to her. Not as suave as I was hoping, but we'll have time for more. "Let's go. I love you, and let's also go, now."

The black girl breathes, starts to stand. I step forward, throw a boot into her stomach. She coughs, grips herself, falls back. I kick her again—I don't know why. She lifts a hand, starts to scream, so I stomp her face. The back of her head cracks the ground, and she rolls to her side, holding her nose. Blood runs between her fingers and down the back of her hands, like leaking paint, dripping off her wrists and onto her legs. She whimpers and breathes.

"Hey, over here." Jennifer waves a hand to me. She stands at the other end of the alley, light blooming behind her like from an open door to heaven. I nod to her, lift my camera, and snap a picture. "Sorry," I breathe over my shoulder as I hurry to my girl.

Jennifer dashes down the street, looking back at me, laughing. Opening her arms to the night air and squealing. Our feet pad the pavement as the gap between us and that alleyway assault widens. I raise my camera and snap pictures of my siren running, arms out, weaving between parked cars and pedestrians. She turns, grins, laughs, and calls to me. She continues to walk backward as I jog to her. A few more pictures, and our bodies become close. I take a final photo of that close up face, radiating moonlight and joy. She closes her arms around me. I smell her hair. She kisses my neck.

"I've been waiting for you," she whispers.

"How do you know me?" I ask into her hair.

"I know that you follow me," she goes on. "It's flattering. I've never been followed before. I've never had someone care enough about me to actually do that."

"Well, I do care about you. I care all about you."

"Did you mean it when you said you love me?"

"Of course I do. I love you."

"I love you, too."

We kiss in the middle of the empty street. I inhale that other girl's odor and swallow it, so Jennifer won't be subject to it any longer. She grins like she never did with anyone else. She grips my hand again, and we weave between the buildings and farther into the night.

"Why did you choose to follow me?" Jennifer asks, watching my hand swing with hers while we walk. "I mean, there are a lot of prettier girls out there. Why didn't you flatter them with that camera, with those eyes? Why pick me?"

I squeeze her hand, so her eyes raise and match mine. "You are radiant. You are special. I don't pick the people I follow; they pick me. You just have this way about you. This effortless perfection cut with a broken damsel in need of someone to set you free."

"Are you going to set me free?"

I hold her cheek. We kiss again.

"I will. I'll do whatever I can, whatever there is. I will make you whole again."

Jennifer presses her head to my chest. I run my fingers through her hair like I wished I could a million times. The fabric of her hair hangs soft and smooth. My fingers melt through the strands, finding the small of her back and holding her gently. I kiss her head. We hold no words, the silence filling us.

"So, now that you have me," Jennifer starts. "Will you still follow other people around?"

My breath stops a moment. The cold drips into my stomach. My hands stiffen against her. I lick my lips, but my mouth dries out, anyway. I grunt and try for words, but I'm not sure what to say. "Well, not the way I followed you. Obviously not. But this, this is kind of my life's work. It's important. It means something. It means everything."

"Why?" she asks, her eyes staring large holes through my head.

"It just is." I shrug. "One day everyone will understand that. It can't be described in words. But I can't stop, not now. Not after all this time."

"How much time?"

"Too much time."

She pouts. "But what if you find a girl prettier than me?"

"There aren't any."

"Can I follow them with you?"

"No," I grunt. I hold my forehead. Her hands drop from my body, and she turns away. I hold out an arm to her. "Come on. If you come, you'll get caught. It's not that I don't want you there, but you know, you have to understand. I just can't have you—" I close my eyes for just a second.

"Will you shut the hell up?" the man shouts.

My eyes open. An old man wearing skin marked in filth and mud sits up in his sleeping bag on the sidewalk. He holds his arms out to me. "Shut the hell up, already. How long do you need to go on about this?"

My eyes scan behind my shoulders, and then in front of me. The streets run empty in all directions. Jennifer stands nowhere. I let the cold breath crawl back out of my throat.

Sometimes you see someone in a crowd. Different features throw themselves at the right angle and out of the corner of your eyes you make it up in your head, and then you go to find that person and say something, and you realize that the person you were looking for is nowhere to be found. And you feel foolish, because of course they wouldn't be there. You are not their crowd. This isn't their scene. You feel dumb for a second and then move on with your life. That happens to me sometimes.

Forming the people I want out of whatever bodies and features I spy, I'm used to creating people I know from strangers' forms. Sometimes, I get a bit too caught up in my art.

"Fuck," I mutter, and I leave the man to his sleeping bag.

I slide against my own secluded corner of the city just as the sky burns grey with the first light of the early morning. I pull out my camera and tap through photos on the screen. I shake my head. What a wasted night.

Delete. Delete. Delete.

Pictures of walls, streetlights, empty cars, nothing at all. There's one photo of the stretching street that I remember from my faded imaginings. I thought our bodies were so close, that I can almost make the outline of her grin through the picture. I run my finger over it, even if she's not there.

Delete.

I come at last to the picture of a black girl holding her bloody face on the ground. Another woman kneels to hold her up, her white skin stained yellow as if with iodine, her blonde hair tied tight on the top of her head, showing the black roots underneath. Her eyes watch me in the photo, her lips scowling in contempt. Her arms are meaty and her fingers thick. How could I ever mistake her for my Jennifer?

But I guess that's how everyone feels when they see the mistake they've made.

I continue to run through each picture, the shadows, the two butch lovers walking to the corner for their fun, the group at the Cat Club laughing and hollering in the street as a cluster. Not a shade of Jennifer in a single shot.

Delete. Delete. Delete. Delete.

Cinderella

I know the feeling well, the sense that someone, somewhere, though you can't put your finger on it, has their eyes on you. I've never experienced it, personally. But I know its signs; I know the shiver, the nervous glance. That way you half-laugh at the person you're with and tell them that you just got a chill; the place gives you the creeps. Well, that chill is usually me. I'm that creep. I'm the one that's watching you.

But tonight I feel it. I glance over my shoulder, looking for someone to be staring back at me. A serpent of a chill slithers its way up my spine, diggings its fangs into my shoulder, forcing me to jerk my eyes around the alley into the dark behind me. But there's no one there. The feeling makes my legs want to dash from the alley, to find a different corner to plant myself. But I can't, because tonight I'm already busy giving a pair of lucky souls the same feeling that I just got.

Plus all my equipment's set up.

"We need to find a hotel," the woman hunkered under a red coat—Alfani, maybe. Nothing special—says as she peers down the street. I'm calling her Jane.

Her man in a black American Rag coat, tapping at his cell phone's screen like a bird on a tree, grimaces. "I'm trying," he complains. "But I don't have any signal. Who the fuck can't get a signal in a city?" This man is so much skin and bones that there's no noteworthy form to him. I'm calling him John.

Jane paces a few steps, turns, paces back. She looks up to the roofs and over the windows. Her eyes pass my shadow, and just as they do, her shoulders jump with a strike of cold, as if she's feeling the presence of a ghost. She drops her eyes to her feet, and turns her face to John. "We should just walk around. I'm sure we could—"

"Or not. We could find ourselves walking into the projects for all we know," John snaps back. He holds his phone out with one hand, while the other spreads open towards the buildings beside them. "You don't see any tourists wandering around here do you? It's got to be all drunks, homeless ones, beggars. You don't want to get raped, do you? I don't."

"No one is going to rape you."

"No, they'll just mug me, stab me, piss on me as I lie dying. Thanks a lot."

"Shut up," she says.

While they turn their backs to each other, I still haven't snapped a single shot of them. What is there to snap? I wonder to myself, two anybodies arguing in the middle street at night? I have old film rolls packed with this shit. Back when I didn't know any better. No point in wasting a valuable SD card storage on it.

I guess my heart's not really in the work tonight. It's been a while now, no good follows. I should sleep, but I don't. I guess that makes me sort of a workaholic.

Then there's this feeling again, a chill resting on my shoulder, prying at me to get in. Shit, I cringe. I turn, pointing my Canon down the alley, shooting off a picture with my flash. The tight walkway explodes in white.

"I'm just going to call us a cab," he says.

"What was that? Was that a gunshot? I came from there." she says pointing my way as my headphones crackle.

And now I've made myself known. It really is an off night.

I press my back against the wall to check the photo on the camera's tiny screen. I know that the pair is too afraid to come check on me in their suspicions. No one ever investigates what could be a gunshot, anyway, don't ask me why.

"Don't be so dramatic. It was probably just a car passing."

"Don't call me dramatic."

"How could it be a gunshot, it didn't even make a sound."

"They have silencers."

"Who has silencers?"

The recorder clicks off as my storage fills up, and my headphones hum to silence. The viewer on the camera lights my face as I squint into the tiny screen, its colors burning lava lamp shapes onto my retina. The shot is of the overexposed bricks across the way pooling white, the ground beneath running from white to grey to black in the distance. The light travels from my flash travels down the alley and weakens to a point at the back, where shadows fill in the open spaces. The suddenly, as if I was expecting it, in those shadows, I catch sight of a length of shimmering blonde hair and a pale hand, half-exposed. Chilling as it is, like I'm actually seeing a ghost, I know that this is a picture worth keeping, and that my night just got interesting.

I hear an engine rumble, doors slam, and a cab carry my nondescript couple away. Maybe if the cabbie decides to mug and murder them on the way to the hotel, like the man had wished for, I'd be missing out. But then that'd be more about the cabbie than it would be about them, and I don't give a rat's ass about cabbies.

Instead, I stare down the alley as I slowly move my body around to get a better view its end. Did my flash scare my pursuer off? Why would anyone be pursuing me? Maybe she's just someone lost, or a street person. Maybe I'm invading her space. Or maybe my eyes tricked me, something about the light flashing against the walls. I check my screen again, zoom, following the curve of the fingers, the arm, the blonde bangs. That has to be someone. I'm not always that crazy.

I hold my breath and wait, watching down the alley. My eyes start to imagine flashes of white as I stare into the darkness for too long. But there's no movement, and the feeling of being watched is gone. I must have scared whoever it was away.

Well, damn. Now I feel like I'm missing out. I didn't even know that I was being followed long enough to enjoy it. I stand up, stretching out my legs, twisting my hips. My bones pop and crack, with my own grunts following. Age never works with a moving body, only one crunched down in the shadows. I kick my legs to course the blood back into them, pack my equipment, and stroll out into the light of the street.

A boring fucking night.

When I was a kid, I remember that the streets were much longer, the buildings much taller. I didn't have a map of the city, with every corner and path scratched into my skull like I do now, but being small, there was more adventure to the city, to seeing what passing from building to building, or turning the next bend would reveal. There was more exposure in the day, people who could really hurt you, more mystery in the night. How young was I you ask? Too young to be alone, that much I know.

But I didn't stay home—not most days, and certainly not the night—so I took to the streets. I have so many pictures of buildings at crane angles during the day, of streetlamps and neon signs at night. I shot the birds of the bay when I was bored with people. Now I care so little I couldn't care less for the architecture of the city, of the nature, of the bay, now. I only care for the people, because they are the changes. I miss having that wonder for every close up of a brick and the shadow of scrap of metal. I miss that need to catch every detail of light. I'm guessing that age corrodes our spirits, even if we don't want it to, and especially if we don't mean for it to.

A bird twitters in the rotted tree the city planted a decade ago and never maintained. It's a tiny, brown bird, pecking at its own feathers. I lift the camera to my eye, step one foot back to get a stable shot.

There was a time I thought I'd be a nature photographer. This was when mom and I would walk the town, not during my later nocturnal strolls. She bought me disposable FunSaver cameras and told me that if I kept practicing someday I would be in a magazine.

White light plumes from my camera, and the bird squawks and flies from the tree. Ashamed, I lower the camera. Shit, I had the flash on. I check the picture on the screen. The light blinds the scene, and the bird, already a blur, half in flight, is overexposed. I still need more practice if I'm ever going to be a nature photographer.

I had a collection of single use cameras, Kodak FunSavers, Fuji Utsurun, Konicas and others. Dad never paid to get them developed. Instead he would holler at my mom about wasting all that money on me to buy them in the first place. She told me she hoped those cameras would help me get out of where we were. In a way, she was right, and they did.

Suddenly a foot claps the sidewalk behind me. A shadow pushes across the street, cast by the streetlights. I hold my breath. Maybe someone really is following me. I catch another flash of that blonde hair peeking from behind a wall. My body twists, and my legs start to run before I know to think. I guess this is just their common response. Maybe this is why people run from me, even when I'm not trying to stalk them. Or maybe it's the other way around and I stalk people, even when I'm not trying.

I run. My shoes pound the sidewalk; my fists jut in front of me and pull back. I heave long breaths and hiss them out. I glance over my shoulder, and I don't see a thing but pools of light shining down and black walls running between them. Just because I can't see them, doesn't mean there can't be someone there, some figure keeping close to me and staying careful. Maybe he (or she) is taking back ways, catching my progress down alleys. Sweat streaks the side of my face. I twist my neck and stare down each passing walkway. The strangled light from the sidewalk flashes the blonde hair and pale skin into my mind. Maybe I'm just crazy. It isn't the first time my mind made up something that wasn't there. But I'm sure the camera saw this figure. The camera never lies.

My legs are going to fall off and my lungs are blowing back smoke. I think I should stop, and so I do. I bring my feet to a heavy halt with a clop in the center of a desolate four-way intersection. I peer in all directions, gasping and heaving breath. Maybe the night's just too boring. Maybe I'm just making shit up for the excitement. All I know is that I don't really know for sure, and not knowing is never really enough, is it?

Now, in my defense, I have been chased more than a few times before, but it's been a while, my body isn't used to the stress. My head falls between my legs, the air tasting better down there. I'm not sure why I'm so terrified at the thought of someone following me, but I am. What's the worst they could do to me? Kill me? That would be no great loss. Maybe it's more the question of why would anyone would bother to follow me. I'm the follower. I'm a person of no importance eve if there is this warmth in my stomach, this pattering in my heart, this nagging thought in the back of my head that maybe I am important. Maybe I do deserve to be followed, and I just don't know it yet.

But I know that's bullshit, so I ignore it.

Whatever the case, my pursuer is gone, and I will probably never know if, or why, I was pursued, and that's probably for the best.

Just as I'm finishing my thought, a single step snaps behind me and it wracks my spine.

"So, that is what you were doing," a voice, girlish but with a slight crackle, says.

Goosebumps run along my arms. There was someone watching me, and I did feel it. I hold my breath and turn on my heels. I see the blonde and pale girl, like an apparition under moonlight. She's wearing a grey sweater, sleeves rolled up, and jeans. All filthy and torn. Her hair is tangled, but her skin is perfect. She looks to be around thirteen, the same age that I started spending my nights wandering city and its back alleys instead of sleeping.

"Who are you?" I ask her.

She smirks. "Why, are you afraid?"

"Not afraid, just surprised. Are you looking for someone? Are you lost?"

She peels her lips back. "I've found who I'm looking for."

My heart skips, my breath holding in my throat. I try to mouth words, but none come. What does she want? Does she want to have sex with me? Did she see me one night and has been following me and tracking me and now confronts me, because she really wants to fuck me? Are Leon's cosmetics working that well? She's young, but not too young. I would be okay with that.

"Were you taking pictures that night?" she asks.

Air bubbles in my throat. "What night? I-I take pictures every night."

"The night my dad was burned alive?"

I have to think. How many pictures of burning people do I have? Not a lot, but enough.

"Was this recent?"

"Are you crazy?" she asks, and I save my response. "You don't remember? You were there. I saw you. I saw you taking pictures of us."

I shrug.

"In the car, a month ago."

"Oh," I jab a finger at her. "Right. Yeah, yeah. Wow. Yeah," I laugh.

The parking lot orphan is who's been giving me chills all night. Had she been following me ever since her dad died? Does she know that it was I who saved her? Does she want me to be her new dad? No, no I can't do that. If she does, she'll be disappointed. She looks so different now, standing here tall next to me. Out of the car and out on the town. It's like a Cinderella story. Well, sort of. Not really. But still.

"I thought it was you that killed my dad."

"Really?" I laugh, feeling like I'm meeting an old friend. "No. I mean, I watched him die, but there's a difference. No, no. He did that to himself."

"He killed himself?"

"Yeah, I guess he was—you know—unhappy."

Her bluster evaporates. She drops her eyes, and pushes her hair back. Silence weighs her down. She throws an eye at me. "Do you have proof?" she asks, voice ringing empty in the night. "On the camera?"

"Oh. Yeah. Yeah, of course."

We find a wall to rest our backs against. I turn the camera away from her to start. "Sorry," I grunt, "but there are a lot of things on here you can't see. No one's allowed to see. Not yet. They're just not ready."

"I only care about my dad."

"Coming right up."

I flick through the pictures. If it was a month ago, it'll take some scrolling. I lick my lips, try at small talk. "You were really good at following me. I'm, you know, impressed. I see a bit of myself in that." I don't tell her that I think she probably made a good daughter.

"Oh." She looks at herself, tapping her finger on the side-walk. "I didn't know how to get you, and I thought maybe you were going to kill that couple you were following." She lets a breath go. "So I bought a knife, but I wasn't sure if I could use it."

I huff a dry laugh. "Well, I'm glad you didn't." My screen scorches with a man on fire, and I turn the viewfinder to his daughter. "That's your dad, right?"

She holds the camera in both hands. Her mouth drops. Her eyes don't break from the screen.

"That is your dad, right?" I repeat.

"Yeah," she croaks. "Yeah, that's him."

"Cool."

I flick through each picture of him, giving her time to absorb every one. I stop where his skin glistens with gasoline, and he's just scraped his match on the side of the building. The fire already glows and throws purples and greens through the igniting fuel.

"You see?" I say. "He made himself into a burning man all on his own."

She nods. She closes her eyes, opens them again, and breathes. "He didn't leave a note."

"Sometimes they don't."

"I guess so." She lets me take my camera back and I replace it into my bag. She stares off for awhile, holding herself. It's about to reach midnight for this Cinderella of the streets, I can tell.

"So." I pause. "Do you—I mean, I'm not sure if I should ask but—do you want to have sex with me?"

She shakes her head.

"Okay." I nod, neck jerking. "I understand. It was just this vibe I got. I just needed to be sure. I've never been followed before."

"But you follow people." She sniffs. "Do you just do this every night. Just follow people around and take pictures of them, hoping to get some gory details?"

"Well, it doesn't have to be gory, but yeah, I guess so," I shrug.

The sun is starting to rise to our sides, throwing blue into the sky and white across us. My Cinderella wipes her eyes on her sleeve.

"They want me to stay with my mum. Thing is, I don't know what I'm doing, where I'm going. I don't know who I'm supposed to be. I thought maybe getting revenge on you would give me something to do, but now not so much." She runs out of words to say.

"Yeah, I'm sure." And I don't have any more for her. I don't want her to think I'm going to take her in. I won't be her brother, or her dad. That isn't happening.

I didn't know where to go, or who to be, when I was alone. When my mother stopped buying me those cameras or playing along with my dreams. When she sleepwalked past me in the night, not feeding me or clothing me. When she didn't watch me or want me. She had lost a son and didn't care that I was the one that was left. I was invisible to her. I was a no one. I was paint chipping off a wall, or a loose floorboard that no one fixes. So, I took to the streets, where I wouldn't want to be seen, and where I couldn't be found. I just wanted to watch. At first to see the birds, then to see the bay, then to see families that even if they weren't happy at least were together and looked at one another. These were my first follows. But no matter who I followed, no one would take me in. I never was the one they wanted. I wasn't their son. I wasn't anyone's son. So, I wandered alone. Hoping to find someone, when I couldn't even find myself.

I'd spend my nights sitting in front of store displays, Macy's, Sears, American Eagle, Nordstrom. All these mannequins, bodies, forms, the suggestions of people. I could make them into whatever I wanted. And they never walked away. They didn't ignore me, because I decided they didn't. They loved me and took care of me. Models in pictures, captured with smiles, hands draped over knees, sitting in cars, sun high overhead. They were my paper-thin friends. They were my kind of people. All the people I'd ever need.

I don't tell her any of these things. I doubt they would make her feel better.

She pats my shoulder, mutters, and stands, sliding the knife into her jacket pocket. She slaps her sides, turns to me, and says, "Well, if you're not the man who killed my dad, then I guess we're done here."

"Are you going home?" I ask.

"I don't have a home," she says as she runs her sleeve under her nose. "I don't have a dad. I don't have a life." She starts to choke on her words. "I guess I'm just going to walk."

I open my mouth. I should stop her. She could turn out like me. Kids always turn out like their parents. But she turns her back, and I don't say a word. I watch her walk away from the warmth of the sun, down the street, between the buildings, and out of sight. I'm sure she'll find her way. She's too smart to be like me. But maybe there was a time that I was too smart, too. I was on my way to being someone, and I'm sure she's on her way, too.

Loss can make us lose our way, even if we didn't want it to, and especially if we didn't mean for it to.

John, Jane, and Mick

When you're strolling through back alleys, minding your own business, you try to step over the rats clawing from the mud, pressing their fat stomachs through pin-sized holes between bricks. You can curl your nose against the usual stench that trails between the buildings. You can try to keep your eyes away from the ground, because you never want to know what you're stepping in. You can watch the bricks scroll past, and your eyes may fall on a half-open dumpster with something hanging over the lip. It's then that you notice it's a hand—a hand gone grey and green. You'll peer in a little closer, and you'll see a woman's face, her eyes wide, mouth pulled into a grotesque scream. Flies will darken her face like crawling moles. You'll want to vomit, but if you're like me, you'll take a picture instead.

Maybe not the last part. Not so much for the average pedestrian, but then the average pedestrian would think better than to slink between the mold stained walls where the liquor store meets a pawn shop on a dark night when the wind whips down every corridor in the city. But that's me, and I'm the one who found her, so I got to do what I wanted with her, photographically at least.

The woman herself was nondescript. This looked to be true even before she was apparently killed and shoved into the dumpster. Even then I doubt she had much in the way of noteworthy features. Makes me wonder why anyone would choose to kill her in the first place. A Worthington black dress, fake pearl necklace, nothing that attests to much in the way of income or class. Neither does the red coat she lies across. Maybe she was his thrill kill. Still I photograph this Jane Doe, if only because I'm interested in how it looks when a person's skull falls apart from blunt force trauma, and not so much because of the body beneath and certainly not because of the soul that had long since escaped.

Parts of her cheek are already peeling off, festering with maggots, some having grown to flies and are now hovering over the rest of the trash in search of a more interesting meal. I take a picture of her ear – she's missing one, and the hole that was left runs from ash to green to yellow to red to black on down into the rabbit hole of her skull. The rainbow of decay captures my photographer's ur-spirit.

From the corner, I catch sight of another person hiding deeper in the dumpster. A pair of white eyes watch me from the dark as I take my shots. I lift the other half of the dumpster lid up, and streetlight shines on another face buried in garbage. This time it's a man. Like with her, I have nothing to note about him. I guess they were made for each other.

Like hers, his face has fallen apart, but with the insects having eaten a gash across his nose. I guess whoever murdered them shattered it before finishing the deed. They each hold sad smiles slashed across their throats, their new lips seeping crimson that pools against brown. I snap a photo that nicely fits both of their mangled faces into a single frame. Mister and Missus John and Jane Doe. The Does, ladies and gentlemen. They were definitely a couple, who else would have them?

Wandering from the dumpster, from the pair of corpses, and into the light and fresher scent of the street, a faint memory glints in the back of my head. I think I recognize these two. They could be anyone, but they are not, something does stir in me. Not too long ago, they fought over who would get raped in a dark alley way and climbed off into a cab together. I guess I should have followed them - that would have led me to someone of note.

Huddled beneath the dumpster, I swipe my camera from one picture to the next and next, sifting through my past and looking for something that I'd never have noticed. I find my way back to Cinderella walking through the dark and then, just a few shots further, to where two people are arguing on the sidewalk, wasting the digital memory my camera has to store them. Just one shot when I first set up, before I felt followed, before I decided that they weren't worth the energy. There, down the road, at the corner, at the edge of the frame, a car was waiting. This is long before they called the cab. I pinch and zoom, and the display pulls the car into full focus without pixel of resolution lost. I stare through the waiting cab's windshield, and I can see the cabbie's face. He is bald, his eyes sunken into their holes, a gnarled nose hooked down so that it pecks his plump lips. Now there's a face any man won't forget. There's someone worth following. Now it's all a matter of finding him. I head uptown to the bars where rich kids drink themselves stupid, then hail a cab to shuttle them home. The cars with morally-loose drivers wait there for the call from dispatch to pick the drunks up, beat them senseless, steal their shit, and abandon them near the projects. It's right where a killer would stalk, I'm sure of it.

Me, I've never killed anyone before. No one's ever paid me enough menace to build that requisite desire to end a life, but sometimes maybe that's not all it takes. Sometimes, if the right body passes and I get this shiver, then I imagine making friends with this strange person, following him or her home over the course of several nights, and then I imagine pretending to hurt myself, and that I'm in need of this person's help, and when that person lets me in and lets me spend the night, I fish a knife from the kitchen, and I jam it in his or her chest, and I watch the life run form this stranger's eyes. I have no idea why I think this, but I do.

I have known one person who's killed someone. My dad, and the only person he really killed wasn't born, so I'm not sure if that counts. He did try to kill my mom while he was at it though, so I guess it still fits the mindset. Besides, the courts decided that he was a murderer. He was rolling thunder of chaos, lightning strikes of violence, that much I can agree with. You could see the sky darken wherever he went and feel his weight pull the air down. When he breathed, people around him held their breath. People would try their best to disappear, but he would always notice them. Not like people notice other people. Like someone would notice a wall to drive holes into. And that is exactly what he did.

They told me that sort of violence comes from drinking, or it comes from drugs. And yes, my old man drank, but only once or so a week. And he smoked, but only cigarettes. I never saw him snort or inject anything, so I'm not sure if that's really the thing. I just think some people are born with a need to hurt, like they came out of the womb missing some part of their brain, and they have to lash out at everyone who has it to try to prove that they're as much a person as we are, even when they are not.

In my town, every cab is colored for a different day of the week. I stalk past yellow and white cabs, and green and blue ones. Even pink SUVs have little light up taxi signs on their roofs. Several of them sit parked at the sidewalk near the bars just before last call, cabbies inside sleeping, talking or masturbating on their phone, or just straight-up drinking. Some even just wait and watch, tapping their fingertips on the wheel, lost in whatever torrent their mind carries them through.

I find the one white cab with my man with the hooked nose parked in the lot next to a tavern. I crouch and slink in as much shadow as I can find. I'm gravel; I'm concrete; he won't see me if I'm gravel or concrete.

And he doesn't. He's the staring ahead type, tapping then chewing on his fingernails and spitting the little pieces of nail out. I can see him watch his own eyes cast against the windshield in the dark. Up close, I feel a dark cold fall off him, the kind that would run ants over my skin if he caught eyes with me through his rearview mirror to where I am hiding. I name him Mick. He looks like a Mick; and he feels like a Mick. Besides, that's the most of a name you could get out before a man like that would kill you.

No one's ever tried to kill me. Even my dad, for all his fury and violence, never tried his hand at ending my life. I guess out of everyone in our family, I was the least worth it, the only one that slinked around. But that's all right. Being no one helps sometimes. Just as I hope it will tonight. I'm not ready for a dumpster coffin, maybe someday, but not tonight.

The hooked nosed cabbie's lights flash on as the doors to the tavern swing open, his engine rumbling as his wheels drag the vehicle onto the road.

A varsity guy, sports jacket and hair sticking up in gelled spikes, laughs and sways with a young Asian woman under his arm. They twist toward the cab as it arrives and open the doors. The pair climb in, a moment passes, and the cab rumbles away. I dart across the street to where a pink SUV lays in wait, and I jump in the back.

"Hey," the cabbie shouts at me. "You need money to ride."

I rustle through my jacket pockets for a pair of balled up twenties, and I hand them to him. I point ahead to the white car showing its read lights down the dark path away from the center of tonight's action. "Follow that car," I say, leaning forward next to the cabbie, feeling like a detective out of a pulp paperback. Those same afternoon crime dramas my mother absorbed herself into every day, cradling the stomach that no longer held my brother. I'm to be the hero from one of her stories, if only for as long as I sit in this cab. The driver follows at crawl, his lights off. If the car wasn't pink, we'd be invisible.

"If he goes farther than a forty, I'm throwing you out," the driver tells me.

"Just follow," I grunt, feeling more grizzled by the second. I'm chasing down a killer. I basically am a hero. I mean, I have no intention of calling the police or arresting him myself, but still, I basically am.

The white cab turns the corner and pulls down an alley along a line of abandoned shops that houses shattered windows and the homeless. My car stops on the side of the road. The cabbie looks back at me to see what he should do. I hold up a hand to say "Wait."

"You smell like shit. That smell had better not stay in the car."

"Shut your mouth, "I tell him.

A long minute passes. Then another. I think I hear a girl scream, but it could just be a passing car, its belts loose. The cabbie drums his fingers on the wheel, glancing back at me. Soon, an engine rumbles, lights show up again, and the white car pulls back around the corner, where it drives down the road. The only silhouette that shows through the rear window is Mick's own, Varsity and the girl aren't with him.

The car twists down the ramshackle backroads to where ruined houses stand with broken fences. It pulls onto the overgrown lawn of a house walled with white shingles that have crusted to an ear wax yellow. Mick cuts the engine.

"Looks like he's home," my driver tells me. "That means I'm done. Get out now. I'm keeping the change for the seat cleaning."

I don't care, he's not important, so I climb out, and the driver swings around and sweeps back toward town. But Mick's important, he's ahead in his rundown home, in his white car out front. He obviously only wanted the pair of patrons that he received tonight. He's out of the car now, lumpy body showing against the white moonlight. He's only fat around the stomach, thick arms and a girl's legs. He pulls the taxi sign off the roof of the car and tosses it in the back seat. I crouch between streetlights, my Canon to my eye, zooming in as Mick bends into his trunk. He throws one limp leg over the ledge, then another. He pulls another pair over. He leans deeper in and stands up, cradling both bleeding bodies under his arms. He holds their heft up to his chin. Their necks dribble rivers of blood that paints his arms and soaks his shirt. He holds his face away from the dying as he drags them to the side door of his home. Fumbling for the keys in his pocket, he presses the two corpses against himself with one arm and props them on his knee until he can unlock the door. He throws it open and lumbers them inside, slamming it shut behind him.

I stalk around the back through a thicket of weeds, grass, and choked flowers. His windows stand high, but I find discarded cinderblocks and buckets to build something to stand on. They give me enough height to lift my camera over my head and turn the viewfinder toward myself, like a periscope, so I can see inside. The glass is brown, caked in dust and cobwebs. It looks like it might be the kitchen, but the shot isn't good enough. I know this won't work, not through that window. I step down and look around. I need to be inside if I'm going to get a clear shot of a killer and his prey.

Around the side of the house, a hill runs up against the wall. The bathroom window stands a foot above it. On my tiptoes I test the window with a push. The frame lifts an inch but hitches on the rust and decay. But since it's not locked I shove it harder. It slips up another inch and then another. I gently shake and push unit it reaches the top. My fingers latch around the windowsill, then, as I hold a breath, I jump up and pull, kicking the wall with the tips of my shoes, and hoist a shoulder through the window. I hold myself there steady, pulling one arm through, and then the other. I press one palm above me and one palm below me, and I push myself through into the black bathroom. My body smacks the ground, my cheek scraping the floor, feeling the grit of his unwashed linoleum. I push myself up and sit against the toilet, letting my eyes adjust to the dark.

The streetlight through the open window paints the bathroom in grey colors. It's empty, basic, and looks like it's barely been used in years. The floor and walls are sticky with dust and lint. But there's no smell, not like I was expecting.

I open the door a crack and press my eye to the slit. Lamps throw a beeswax yellow into a living room to my right. The light barely filters down the hallway that connects it to this bathroom. To the left I hear shuffling, or more like scraping, I guess. I press the door open another inch, just far enough to where I can pull a shoulder through the gap. When it's just wide enough, I slide my body through the opening, pressing my back to the wall and crawl across the hallway toward where harsh white light glows.

I'm wallpaper. I'm dust. I'm just another piece of abandoned furniture in the house of a murderer. He can't see me.

Mick is leaning over a basin set on the floor of his kitchen, his back facing me. Professional studio lights have been set at the corners of the room. They are throwing a glare over the white floor, making it seem like he's standing on the light itself. In the center of the room he scrapes at the metal of the basin. He lifts a blade through the air as he works. One pair of pale feet hang over the edge of the basin. In one of the corners, near the kitchen door, the dead girl stares at me in her flashy blue top and white pants. The blood from her throat sticks her top to her chest, staining her pants. I wish her head would turn, fall aside, and stop looking at me. Her stare drives a chill like I've been caught through my spine. I have to remind myself that she's dead, and not to worry. The dead only see what kills them.

I slink back from the kitchen, turning down the hallway, and crossing into his living room. Long drapes block the streetlights through the front window. Two deadbolts and a chain hold the door shut. Only a couch sits in the room. There's no TV, not even a coffee table. A painting hangs on the wall that faces the couch.

It's of a couple sitting at a picnic. I don't get what it means, but I photograph it. I photograph all of it. This is where a killer lives. This is the home of a man who takes lives. It certainly doesn't look like the houses in my mom's old crime dramas.

But I don't look like any of them TV detectives either.

Another hallway runs around the house from the other side and gives way again to the white lights of the kitchen. This time it faces Mick and his body basin. I stay just short of the triangle of light, pressing my body deep against the wall and angling the camera that I can just make out the killer and his work. He is sawing his blade through the young man's stomach. As he digs deeper, he pulls out a handful of intestines. Another cut, and he pulls more out. He wraps the guts around his knuckles, and the blood runs down his wrist. A septic smell seeps into the hallway. He winds more guts, and they wrap it across his wrist and down his arm. His eyes hold the body, where he stares with the same open-eyed intensity as he did at his windshield when he was preparing himself for this kill. When he finishes with the intestines, he drops them into the basin, and he saws into the chest. More blood runs down his arms, and a fresh blast of copper hits the air. Mick works his bloody hands like a surgeon, like an artist, like someone so entrenched in his work that he can't pull himself free. I don't see my father in this killer. None of the rumbling fury, none of the strikes of violence. Just work. Just passion.

After he saws free the heart out of the young man, he holds it in his hands, his fingers trembling. He lifts the organ up to his eye-level, and he looks at it in a way that I know no one has ever looked at any part of me. His mouth hangs open as he holds his breath. He turns and walks with this prize to a mason jar he's already prepared on the counter. His hands drop the organ in the fluid inside the glass, and he seals it shut. Then, he lifts the young man out from the basin and folds his empty body in half, leaving it in the corner of the room.

Mick then takes the young woman in his arms and carries her to the basin. He lays her in and begins the same work. He does it with such detail, such craft, I'd say almost with a love, , but I'm not sure of the intricacies of this love. All I know is that if I ever were to be a killing man, I'd want to kill like he kills.

When he's finished, he washes his hands, takes each body, folding them under his arms, and walks them out to his car. I watch through the side door window as he tosses them into his trunk and drives off, probably to drop them in some dumpster at some forgotten corner of the city as well. Two more faces only to be seen from now on in the newspapers.

On the counter the two mason jars stand like two soldiers. Behind them rows of more hearts stand. I count them. Sixteen in all. They share the counter together, holding their prized places in the white studio light. They all look the same to me, brown and swollen, floating at the bottom of some liquid, but each one has a masking tape label slapped onto it. Each label with faded pen-drawn words that I can barely make out or understand.

"Holy house." "Bus tickets." "Maiden name." they say.

Seeing as how they're set up to be photographed I shoot each jar, and when finished I wander freely through the house. It is a small building, a single story, and the only room I haven't entered is the bedroom off to the side of the living room. Inside, it's dark, dingy, the floor matted with piles of clothes. The light switch doesn't work. Flies swarm the clothes, and I can smell the dried blood pulsing off each article of cloth. I curl my nose, and push my feet on ahead. I step over the discarded rags he wears when he kills, and I lie down onto his bed. It's soft. I hold my arms out, my legs apart, the beginning of a snow angel. There are no lumps, no springs. It's blissful. I close my eyes and dream.

This is the bed a killer sleeps in.

I fall asleep without meaning to. But if you were in that bed, you'd understand. You'd probably fall asleep too.

I wake up to the low growls and grumbles of a throat in the dark. I've balled myself into a fetal shape at the corner of the bed, tucked up against the wall, while I slept. A heavy body weighs down the side next to me. His shoulders rise and fall as he mutters and snores. I hold my breath, feeling like a little boy again, caught by his father. But this killer doesn't move. He sleeps.

Didn't he see me? Doesn't he care? Why didn't he kill me? Then I remember, the light doesn't work. He was probably too tired to notice after his work. Maybe he just didn't see. How does someone pass out without noticing another body in his bed? I ask myself.

I stand over him and step off them bed. My bag is at the foot of the bed. My footfalls are silenced by the mounds of crumpled clothing while I cross the room to the door. It stands wide open to the living room. I step through and press myself to the wall beside it to catch my breath and my thoughts.

The killer in the bedroom snores on. I didn't wake him.

As I stand there legs start to quake, my fingers to twitch, the march through the kitchen and out the side door to the streets and the night air feels almost impossible. I could have died back in that bed. I could have been a heart in a jar with some nonsense scrawled over my label. Only when I'm three blocks away does the breath come back to my chest. I counted. I feel that I should have been a part of a serial killer's collection. Maybe once he would have gotten caught. Maybe then I would have been famous.

I can hear the newscaster now. "Police say that one of victim's heart appears to belong to the owner of a bag containing some bizarre and disturbing pictures and recordings. Police aren't sure what to make of it. We'll now show you a few of the images found, but we must warn our viewers that some of these sounds and images may be disturbing."

A smile pulls at my cheeks at the thought, but it falls, because I'm walking the streets, and I'm certainly not dead, which means I won't be famous. I'll never be important. At least not tonight. Maybe not ever.

The reason Mick didn't hack me to pieces is because he didn't notice me. I was a pile of clothing on the edge of his bed, pressed up against the wall. I wasn't a person. I never am. My heart sinks as I realize this. So would yours.

He would never have killed me, because he would never have looked at me the way he looks at those hearts he collects. Like how my dad stared at the wife he hated, the coming son he feared, but like how he never saw me as anything more than just a body in his space. Just a space filler. A tear runs down my cheek. No one will kill me, because they think I'm already dead. Maybe I should think about killing myself, but I wouldn't know how to photograph it, and if I can't document my own death, then how will it make me famous? No one will be there to document it for me. So I can't kill myself. Not now.

I wander the dark until the lights rises up in the sky, until mid-morning when I reach an alley and a dumpster that smells of more than the usual decay. I squint at the shadow, and just in the notch where the dumpster lid hinges to the body I catch the twinkle of a little pale white toe.

I press my eyes shut, turn, and walk from the alley. I don't want to see them; I don't have time for that, not in this mood. Why did I have to find this alley? I could have walked down any street. I turn the corner and try to control my breathing. Sobs pile up high in my throat. I just can't bear to see someone who's received as much love, attention, adoration, and care as someone who's understood the stinging pleasure of being murdered.

My brother was lucky to die feeling only that one feeling in his whole existence, because a life without that feeling, that feeling of being terrified of dying—a life like mine—is hollow, empty, and wasted.

Big Boris and a Surprise Guest

Normally I make a point not to follow towering, bald men with white wife-beaters stretched over their boulder muscles, sweat soaking the cotton see-through. Especially since this man's face holds eyes that boil rage and a scowl that's begging for a fight. He has fists like bricks, and legs as stacks of cinderblocks. Not the kind of person you'd want to be caught with in a dark alley, so I guess the idea was not to let him catch me.

I don't even know why him, but I don't ever really know why anyone. You'd think that out of all the people shoving around the world at any second, at any point in time, that happens to be on the same street with me, is itself the greatest of coincidences. By that logic anyone I run into is worth following. Besides, it's nearing daylight; and I have the need a follow, or so at least I tell myself. A terrifying motherfucker like him will have to do.

I keep a tail with extra distance in case I need to run as he saunters through the dark. Not that I'd get away. I'm sure he has a gun or knife or some other killing tool to run me down with and end my life. But the danger of the stalk pushes me on. It reminds me of wildlife shows I've seen as a kid, a man in a hat following his dangerous hunt through the deepest jungles, and I can't help but feel that same exotic curiosity those adventurers must have felt.

But unlike them, I have no bushes to hide under, no tree to hide behind, only some urine stained walls. It works fine though, and might even smells about the same. I am urine, I tell myself. I am brick. I will not be caught.

The lumbering beast, I'm calling him Boris—trust me, you'd agree with that name if you saw him too—shifts his weight back and forth down back alleys with the ownership and pride of a rhinoceros patrolling its territory. He leans against a wall at the street corner, arms crossed, sucking on a pipe and blowing white smoke into the air around him. I can see that he closes his eyes while he smokes. I hold a steady distance behind him, my Canon my buffer. I watch him through it like I imagine an Australian Wildman would through a set of binoculars.

I've had plenty of fantasies of playing the adventurer trying to tame the wild beasts, but I know I'm not a kid anymore, and I have no intentions of trying to tame this massive monster.

A scrawny, scraggly man in a dirty, torn T-shirt runs up to Boris, jerking his arms around in quick motions, running his jaw, his eyes flashing wild, sweat greasing his face. I snap a shot of what I guess is terror screwing up his eyes and twisting his mouth. I can't hear what they say, and I don't have the time to assemble my mic, so I can only watch and imagine what he's saying.

"Shit, man," I see the small guy ramble. "Shit, shit, shit, shit, shit."

Boris sets a hand around the man's shoulder, pulls the pipe from his mouth. "Calm down. Shut up. What do you mean?" his voice the sound of a cement mixer.

The scraggly man points down the street. "I did it bad. I fucked up. Bad, bad, bad, bad, bad, man. Bad, bad, bad, bad, really bad."

Boris grips his other shoulder forcing the scraggly man to tremble harder under his hold. "Calm the fuck down before I crush you to powder and snort your bones." Or something like that, I'm sure. "What bad did you do?"

The scraggly man looking over his shoulder again mouths, "The really bad kind of bad."

Boris grimaces and drops his arms. The man twists his spine, points behind himself, and moves in quick steps down the road. Boris watches him for a while. He sucks a final drag on his pipe, and with his eyes closed blows the smoke toward the sky, then follows.

My camera swinging over my neck and my pack strapped to my side, I pursue them under shadows and the night's sky.

As he runs ahead, the scrawny man's sneakers clap the sidewalk. Glancing over his shoulder he catches sight of Boris lumbering behind him. I keep half a block back, sticking to walls and corners pretending that the light from the street lamps would burn me if I touch it. The Canon keeps them in sight. I hunch, curling myself up child-sized as I follow.

The two men weave down blocks of empty buildings, rundown and abandoned by all but the homeless. I see small fires burning behind windows with their glass missing. Suspicious men and women dressed in clothes fitted for a different body mill around the fires, chatting to each other and by themselves. I've never felt more at home then I do with these people. No one notices the weird asshole ducking into buildings when everyone's a weird asshole ducking into buildings. I keep my walking at ease and push through to the main road. Empty faces throw me vacant looks as I pass, but no one moves for me. They're all too malnourished, too tired, to put up a fight with someone who at least appears vital. Not that I have any; vitality that is, just don't anyone tell them.

The firelight from an oil barrel fire throws a devil's glow over Boris's back, lighting his heavy steps like the gait of a man leaving the world on fire. I snap a picture to capture the moment, because it feels like the right thing to do.

The scraggly man continues to lead Boris through rows of rundown, 'white-trash' homes each with their own chain link

fences and creaking screen doors. Dogs jump at one fence after another, barking murder. The scraggly man points ahead and leads
on. He opens a fence and leads Boris through. The scraggly man
hurls a rock at the charging dog, smacking him in the snout,
shutting him up. I assemble my mic down the road, half-hidden
behind a large white 'rapist' van. The static of the dogs growling
breaks into the low rumble of their conversation.

Boris clears his throat as he enters the yard. "This is no good.
How did you let this happen?"

"I let the dogs get at her." The scraggly man whips another
rock at the dogs gathering around them. "Fuck off. Get out of
here. Fuck off."

The dogs yip and jump over each other to get out of the
way. They scatter around the fence toward the back of the house.
He scratches the back of his neck, points to the weeds. "That's all
that's left of her."

Boris grunts. "I see that. Might as well let the dogs finish
the job."

"You think?"

"You want anyone other than me to know?"

The scraggly man shrugs, staring at the ground. The grass
is too high, the fence too thick, and the night too dark for me to
make out what they're staring at. I mean, I think it's a dead body
of a girl; I'm not stupid. But whose body exactly seems an important question when something like this falls before you, doesn't it?

"I didn't mean to," the scraggly man whispers.

A dog yips at the back of the house. Others yowl.

Boris slaps the scraggly man's shoulder. "Go out for the
night, leave the dogs to her. In the morning we'll wash up what
they don't finish. Make sure lots of people see you tonight. Make
sure lots of people see you having fun."

The scraggly man nods, not moving his eyes from the de-
pression in the grass. Boris pulls at his shoulder to get the oth-

er man's legs working. They step off, shutting the fence behind them. Boris keeps the scraggly man close while they walk. They whisper to each other.

"Don't worry about it."

"I killed her."

"No, you didn't. You didn't even see her today. Forget about her, she's gone. We'll have a drink instead."

I snap the last of their bodies fading into the night, disappearing down the block into their invisibility. Then, I pack up my mic and skulk across the street to the gate in the fence. I peer over its top for the dogs. I can hear them grumble somewhere behind the house. I glance to the side of the fence where the girl's corpse is supposed to lie, but I can't make out anything from this angle. With a couple quick glances over my shoulders I unlatch the fence and slip through, shutting and locking it behind me. I hold my body low, almost crouching to all fours, to stay out of sight from the street. As with the instinct of a wild animal, I pull myself along the foundation of the house, so that I may be able to disappear. As I crouch, my foot smothers in some dog shit. I tell myself that's all right, it just means that I'm somewhere where no one ever thinks to look.

I'm like the dog shit. I'm grass. I'm nothing.

I peer into the dark, towards the point in the grass where something is glistening, where an outline of some shape I should recognize starts to shows. I squint, my eyes adjusting, and soon I see her. I know she's there because I can already smell the blood, the rotting meat that the dogs have yet to chew and swallow. She has long strands of brown hair running from her smashed skull and one arm lying by itself in the grass closest to me. I try not to believe what I see. I snap a flash picture of that hand to make sure it's really there. Little white swirls run circles over her black nails.

"Oh, hi, Jennifer. I didn't expect to see you here," I whisper.

Her stomach is split, innards dragged out by the claws of the dogs. Bits and pieces of her bloody guts lie scattered in scraps in the grass all the way toward the corner of the fence. Some pieces of her lie just over the fence, where fighting dogs threw it. Her chest didn't fare any better. Gashes from their claws dig trenches down her flesh. Her breasts are red and oozing with bite marks up and down their sides. Her neck runs a crusty red with a deep fissure from where a dog's teeth took hold and tore a chunk free. Her arms are mostly stripped of flesh at this point, just dried blood and bone. Both her feet are missing. I assume the dogs are barking over them around in the back of the yard.

She has the same face, so beautiful, serene, untouched, except for the bullet hole just under her left eyebrow. Her head lies sideways as if it's turning over to look at me. I snap photo after photo of her, capturing every inch of her skin in death as I did in life.

Now more like my menaquinones than ever, she'll be my model until the skin rots off her face.

Why didn't she pick me, I wonder. This is what happens when you choose someone dangerous over someone who deserves you. I could have saved her. I tried to save her. Didn't I try to save her? Or did I just make that up in my head? You saw me right? Everything is running together so much that I have a hard time remembering. Maybe this is what she deserve for not having noticed me. How many times does one have to follow a girl before she finally sees you?

Still, something twists in my guts. A pang strikes me. She's dead. It's really Jennifer and she's really dead. Or maybe I'm just making her up. Maybe it's just the corpse of some common street whore—but that doesn't mean it can't have been Jennifer. She always looked like a lover to me. Still, it could be anyone. I could just be making up the fingernails, the hair. I have to check the camera to make sure. The photos never lie to me.

Same long hair, same pale face, same black fingernails, yes, same dead Jennifer.

I had already known it was her by the way my legs knock together when I tried to walk away. How I tipped over near the opposite side of the fence to my knees and vomited until I could only dry heave slugs of white stomach bile.

I wipe my mouth on my sleeve, trying to stop the hitch in my throat, and stand up holding the fence for support.

I should do something. I need to do something. I need to take some kind of action. I could go to the police. I have photographic evidence. There's no denying that. They'd have to do something, it's their job. They'd have to sit me in one of those brick rooms, and give me coffee, even though I've already had enough coffee. I would tell them that I was wandering by, that I just happened to see these two men shouting about someone being dead. I would tell them that I'm a professional photographer, obviously, so I snapped a few pictures of the commotion, and, when they left, I went to check what all the fuss was about. I'd tell them that I was only in the yard, so as to not be breaking and entering. And that's where I'd tell them I found her. I wouldn't tell the police that I knew her, or that I had followed her, or that I was in love with her. That would surely make me a suspect in their eyes.

I snap a picture of the house, just so they'll know where it is, and another one up close of the address. Then, I scroll through my photos, scouring for the faces of Jennifer's murderer and his unwitting accomplice. My thumb shakes as I swipe through each one. I have pictures of their backs, of their sides, of shadows playing on their faces. Nothing concrete. Nothing substantial. Goddamn my brilliant eye for drama and composition. I have nothing to show the police. And I'm definitely not just backpedaling here, because I realize with each picture I scroll through just how much the police might actually see that I don't want them too.

Sorry, Jennifer. It's not that I don't care about you. It's just that I don't care enough.

A dog's bark breaks from around the side of the house. It runs the hairs up the back of my neck. A dog, some mutt of a handful of deadly breeds, legs thick with a snarling snout, dashes around into the yard as it makes eyes at me. My breath catches in my chest, and I pull up my camera and bag and run up the stairs. The dog keeps pace, and I throw open the screen door to smack its face. It howls and hits with such momentum that it strikes the porch on its side and topples down the stairs. I try to push on the front door, but it's locked, of course. I throw my shoulder into it, and it only rattles. I reach into my bag and fumble for my plastic credit card—not that I ever really use it. The dog stands at the bottom of the stairs watching me, head low, growling a steady thunder. His brothers start trotting around towards him. I try not to think of dog attacks or of how Jennifer's body looked after the beasts had their way with it. I slip the card between the door and the lock and do the quick work of opening the scraggly man's thread bare lock. I throw the door open, step in, and slam it behind me, locking it again, and breathing deep, letting out tiny gasps. Once my heart calms and cools, I take the chance to peruse what must be my Jennifer's last home.

The shallow room stretches out pure black into a void that swallows anything that might fall into it. Slivers of silver glow from between the thick curtains. I may not have mentioned it, but I have a policy about not turning on other people's lights: Power runs up the electric bill. I try to be as considerate as possible when I'm in these situations. Lights also help an intruder get caught, but still my feelings are mostly about saving the people the cents when I have the opportunity to do so. I feel my way past end tables, sticks of furniture and peek out between a pair of curtains. The window overlooks an empty lot and the brick side of a housing project. I pull these curtains open letting the light that can, in. It falls in too thin to give me much in the way of color to what lies around me but enough to discern the general shapes so that I'm not bumping into things. I can make out a flat screen TV on a dresser in the corner, clothes draped over its edges. There's a coffee table in the center of the room covered in old mail, old food containers, and the stubs of joints in a glass ashtray. Burn marks litter the surface. Paper bags and fast food wrappers run the carpet and pile behind a love seat that looks saved from the Seventies, stained and cigarette burnt as well. The room holds together with the sticky scent of spilled alcohol.

I sit on this man's couch and stare at his table. The pizza in the box is still warm, and his beer as yet unspilled. I drape my arm across the back of the loveseat, and Jennifer drops her head into my embrace. She looks up with eyes of a pet waiting for my touch. I run my fingers over the side of her face, stroking her hair. Her lips part as she leans in. I follow her lead. Our mouths connect. Her warm spit leaks down my throat. I leave my eyes open to watch her as she kisses me. She pulls back and smiles. "I love you," she whispers.

"I love you too," I reply.

But the room runs dark and empty except for the garbage, and I'm just sitting there mumbling to myself.

Why did she pick this scrawny fucker? Why him over me? He looks like a wreck of nerves and anxiety, a weak man. A woman like her needs someone better than that, someone quiet, strong and calming, someone like me. But he's who she picked, probably because she thought she was too good for me. She may not have ever really seen or talked to me, but it's just a feeling you get about someone. And I've gotten good at having those feelings.

Still I wish she wasn't dead.

A gunshot ring rattles the house from a car's backfire, and I jump. Thoughts of drive-by gang warfare jumble in my head from a mix of new reports and cop dramas. The thought unnerves me enough to make me stand up, creep to the blinds, shut out the light, and get myself to the door.

I check for the dogs before making my run. They rumble and slurp from a spot in the grass blocked by the porch. But I know where they are. Silently I shut the door, turning the lock before it closes. I tiptoe across the porch, making my way to the edge. I look over the railing and watch the dogs busy at their work again. They slurp and snap their jaws, sucking down the last of Jennifer's innards and skin. I doubt that they've ever been quieter.

I take a chance, and press my feet careful steps down each stair without a creak. My shoes reach the grass, as I grab the gate, throw it open, and slam it shut. One of the dogs looks up, bending its ears back. It matches eyes with me, blowing air from its nose, and lowers its face back into Jennifer's open stomach.

I let a breath run from my throat and lift my camera to my eye and snap one last shot of this girl who could have been mine. Now she's no better than me, just because she didn't want me, all because she pushed me away.

She did shove me away, didn't she? Maybe. I'm not sure. You were there, weren't you?

I walk back down homeless row. A pot-marked guy looks my way and curls his nose. Bug eyes follow me down the way that I came, and my heart strains. Did someone see me? I follow their homeless gaze and looks to see what they see desperately running down the sidewalk. A steady trail of little brown marks follow me. The homeless shake their heads and look away. I forgot that I had even stepped in it.

A little pile of Jennifer, I'll call it.

Silvia

She stands twisting out of place on the street, waiting on the first corner of Squatter Row, a section of street where the dumpsters house fires, and the abandoned buildings house as many human bodies hidden under the floorboards as they do rats in the cellars. Anyone who lands here either doesn't know where they are or have nowhere else to be. This woman, tall and black, hair tied back high on her head, looking over her shoulders, wears a crisp grey denim jacket, Levi's, and slim black pants. She's too trendy, too well put together, to mean to be here. But she doesn't look lost. Her face, all sharp lines, high cheekbones and piercing eyes, play to the thought that she's looking for something. She's searching. But for what?

I call her Silvia, because like with everyone else I name, I think she looks like a Silvia.

As I lean against the wall, I keep an eye on her, my arms crossed, pretending to pay more attention to my knuckles than I do to the strange woman pacing back and forth on a short line on the sidewalk. She doesn't pay me a sliver of mind because I fit in here more than I'd like to admit. She turns on her heel and walks down the street out of my line of sight.

So I wander out from my alley, swaying, trying to look drunk. At this hour, this street is one of the most populated parts of the city. You might not know that at first, since half of its occupants are holed up in the concrete ruins that line either side, laying low from the law or too wasted to move. But a few souls will walk into the air, too blasted to know what they're doing. As long as I feign that blasted look, that mystique of absolute mindlessness, I'll disappear. I'll become smoke from a dumpster fire. Swaying, oblivious, lost in the background.

She glances over her shoulder, catching her eyes with mine, and I fall against a wall, sliding down to sit at its bottom, staring between my legs, hoping she'll overlook me. Crumpled on the ground, I mutter half-words and rock back and forth, waiting for her to continue up the road. It looks like she doesn't pay me a second look. I'm a rat, a cockroach, a pigeon pecking litter in the street. When I'm sure she's not looking at me anymore, I find my way to me feet, making sure to shamble. She turns another corner, and I confident she's already stopped paying attention to me. If there's one skill I've acquired over my years of service in stalking people on these streets, it's to know that people immediately lose interest in me. But to me it's just a means to an ends. Someday everyone will pay attention to me. They'll see what I've seen, and they'll have to take notice. Or maybe that's just something I say to myself to feel better when they don't.

I sway up the street, stumble around a corner, and spin under a streetlight. And it is then that I realize this woman has been paying far more attention to me than I expected. But who could blame me for having low expectations when it comes to something like that? It's always been that way.

Silvia is aiming a gun at me.

It's a black pistol. The streetlights make it shine. She grips it in two hands, her knees bent, arms steady, the killing end of the weapon leveled at my collar bone. This stops my feet, weighing down the breath in my stomach. I sputter a word or two at her, but god knows what they are. My mouth moves without my knowledge. Who the hell is she and why is she pointing a gun at me? Not to say she doesn't have a reason to; I just don't know what they are.

From the walls and corners men in beige uniforms step forward, holding their same pistols on me.

I raise my hands as she barks, "Hands on your head. Your head."

My palms rest on the greasy, dirt choked hair twisting off my head. My fingers intertwine with each strand. I stare ahead as Silvia slips her gun back into her coat and fishes out a pair of handcuffs. I'm going to be arrested? Shit. I know I deserve this. I just don't know how much they know that I deserve this.

The cruisers sit in shadows a block away. Silvia and her faceless men walk me toward it. She stands ahead, with a guy to each of my side in case I try an escape. One fingers the Taser in his holster. You can't outrun electricity, I think. Silvia doesn't read me my rights. "You are not being arrested," she says. "We just want to talk to you. But we will find ourselves an excuse to arrest you, if you give us trouble."

She sets me in the back of one of the cruisers. One of her officers sits beside me; Silvia drives with the another next to her. She glances at me in the rearview mirror, but no one says a word as we drive.

They drop me in a blue concrete room in the precinct's basement. I've never been arrested before. The only time I ever sat in a police station was after my mother was shot. Two men dragged Dad in here, shaking him and shouting. He swung at both officers, and they landed hits across his face and rammed boots into his stomach as payback. He spit blood and screamed and raved right back at them. I remember A middle-aged red haired woman who tried her best to keep me calm. I wept to myself and held my breath to keep from choking on my own sobs. She handed me a cup of instant hot chocolate and told me just to sit and wait, someone would come over and talk to me soon enough. They asked me if I had any grandparents, any aunts, uncles. I told them that I had no one. They drove me to the hospital that night, where I slept in a waiting room chair just outside the ICU where my mother lay dying, and what was left of my baby brother was being extracted from her to be cremated.

An hour after they leave me there, Silvia struts in . There's no clock, and no windows so I can't know for sure. There's only two chairs, a table, a door, and a camera peering down from the corner of the ceiling. She carries in two steaming cups of coffee, sets one in front of herself, and shoves the other across the table to me. I touch the cup, but its heat burns my fingertips so I just stare at it. They took my bag from me when they brought me in. Are they going through my storage devices? Are they seeing everything that I saw, hearing everything I've heard? I'm afraid to ask, because I don't want to draw attention to them. I purse my lips and let a slow breath run from my nose.

Silvia sips from her cup, clears her throat and asks, "So, what's your name?"

"That's the first question they asked me." I don't know why I said that.

"When?"

I shrug. "When I was a kid."

"You were here when you were a kid?"

"Not here, exactly."

"Okay?"

The steam from the two cups of coffee rises up between us. I try to lift my cup, but it still burns my palms. I've been in here, under the air conditioning for too long. The cold is making my shoulders shake, and my skin's too sensitive against the heat of the Styrofoam cup.

"You'll need that to keep you awake. You might be in here for two long days. Either that, or you can just talk to us now."

"Okay." I have a feeling I'm really going to need to this coffee.

"Where do you live?"

My eyes fall, body shifts in my seat. I tap the table. "That's kind of a personal question, don't you think?"

"No, I don't."

"I just—you know—don't want to get on any mailing lists or anything."

"You live on Squatter's Row."

"No. Come on, I have standards."

"You don't look it."

I clasp my hands around the cup, breathing the steam in. I think of all the officers upstairs, flipping through my pictures on their computers. Maybe they'll catch the hundreds of people walking, arguing, of streets and lamp posts, of birds and mammals. Maybe they'll turn it off before they see the shots of the dead corpses and the violence and take them the wrong way.

"Is there a reason why I'm here?" I ask her. The steam isn't helping with the uncomfortable chill of the room.

"You match a description, fit a profile."

"Oh," I say, my hands shaking. I lift the burning cup to my lips, the liquid inside sears my tongue. I gulp, and it boils inside down my throat, splashing my guts. I cough and set the cup down.

"Well, you know, I have one of those faces. I doubt I'm anyone that a person would point out, remember, or recognize, so I can't imagine I match a description."

Silvia sneers. "Of a dirty looking little guy who likes to follow people around?"

"Oh." My heart sinks. "Well that, I don't know."

"Got a couple interesting ones for you. A young, homeless man was sleeping in an alley one night when he noticed another man lurking near what he considered to be 'his' dumpster. He said it was dark, but you—or whoever this culprit is—was fishing around in there, fidgeting. After this man disappeared, the young man went to his dumpster and found two bodies inside. They had been decomposing for a couple days, both had their hearts and in-nards stripped from their bodies. You know anything about that?"

I shake my head. "That sounds like something I'd remember."

She raises her eyebrows, and takes a drink. "Also, we have a fourteen-year-old girl who noticed an odd man matching your description stalking around a parking garage, looking at her and her father, right before her dear old dad burst into flames. That wouldn't be striking any bells for you, would it?"

"No, no, no." I shake my head, waving my hands. "And for that, that girl actually tracked me down herself, before any of you found me. She confronted me, and I was able to satisfy her curios-ity, and she knows that I had nothing to do with any of that. You can just go ask her. I'll wait."

"Well, we'd like to, but she's been missing for a month."

And suddenly I can't think of any words to say. I'm sure I make some sounds, but they don't mean anything to me. Silvia gives me the eyes to let me know that she thinks I'm dead. Well at least my pictures will finally make the news. I'll be plastered across the front pages. Maybe I'll get a book deal in prison. Pris-on shouldn't be much different than the streets. I'm sure I could disappear in there all the same. Or I could become famous like that Charles Manson. I doubt he regrets anything he's done. He's fucking Charles Manson.

"Anything to add?" Silvia asks.

I drag a long breath down and then let it crawl out. Maybe I won't make the news. I won't hit papers. I won't get any fancy prison book deal nor a 2 hour PBS documentary. Maybe I'll just be some killer who splashes the back page of the news in a single issue of the local paper. No twenty-four-hour, around-the-clock countdown to my execution. Especially since I haven't even killed anyone. I've just been a little bit weird. No one gets famous for being weird. I could admit to murdering John and Jane, but I don't have their hearts back at my place in jars, and if they do find the real killer, then I'm just as fucked. And even though I'm actually innocent, I'd end up rotting in jail for being a creepy, strange something-close-to-a-man, accomplice to a couple acts that would make another person a celebrity. But no one ever remembers the trusty side-kicks. Shit, what to do?

Silvia just watches me. I don't know how long it's been since I haven't been talking, and the room gives me no indication of the changes in time.

"You've been sighted around the area more than these couple times, too. We're just trying to put together who you are. Are you dangerous? Are you responsible for anything? All we know is that you're not as good at staying unseen as you obviously think you are."

What a cunt. Why beat a man when you have him cuffed? I've followed hundreds of people. I've been hiding as a hobby for decades. You're not going to tell me how good of a job I'm doing, Silvia. You can't even catch a man who has at least sixteen hearts sitting on his kitchen counter as we speak. How's that for fucking up? Seems a little more desperate than my few slips.

"What did just you say?"

I stare at Silvia like she's staring at me, mingled with confusion and worry. Were my lips moving? I'm not usually around people when I'm thinking, so sometimes a word or two might slip out. I'm getting pretty worked up here. Maybe something escaped. Something more than a little muttering. Shit. Shit. Shit.

"What did I say?" I ask her.

"You tell me what you said."

"I don't know what I said," I sputter shaking in my seat, gripping the edge of the table. "I was just thinking. I didn't think I was speaking. It was just a thought."

"What about hearts in jars?"

"I didn't kill anyone."

"We don't think you killed anyone. But there are other crimes in the world." She leans across the table. "Like withholding information from the police. You can leave here tonight, if you tell me what you meant about hearts in jars."

My heart hammers, my breaths coming out broken. This is what I get for spending time around someone who's actually paying attention to me.

"I was just muttering to myself. I don't know what I was saying."

"We have a room full of corpses missing their hearts. That wasn't just talk." She won't break her piercing eyes away from mine. Even when I look away, her stare just burns into a different part of my head.

"What about those hearts? Do you know the man who is doing this?"

"Not really."

"What do you mean, not really? What do you know about him?"

I start to shake, twisting in my chair. It's so much easier to be a scared kid sipping hot chocolate than a scared man sipping coffee. I hyperventilate. My legs kick out from under the table on their own. The chair falls out from under me, and I smack to the ground. My body spasms, slapping the floor. Silvia stands from her seat, watching me as I writhe. I wouldn't call it a seizure, because I'm pretty sure I can stop myself, that I'm just making myself do this. I just don't want to stop.

The door opens, and two men run in. Silvia raises a hand to keep them back. She steps toward me, holding those eyes on me.

"Don't touch him. Let him work this out. We're close. He knows something."

I continue to slap and shake. My tongue fills my throat, and I choke on it. I gurgle bubbles as I twitch on the ground.

"Silvia," another officer starts.

"He's faking it."

"He'll die."

Silvia leans over me, her head hovering inches from where I slobber and spit.

"My son was found without his guts or heart. Please. This means everything to me. We won't hold you. We won't charge you for anything. Just give me something," she coos.

I stop shaking.

"Fuck," one of the officers shouts. "Is he dead?"

Silvia shakes her head. "No, I think he's ready to talk."

They return my bag, and Silvia and I walk out to the sidewalk, the night air freezing the sweat on my forehead. Faking a seizure sure takes a lot of effort, it uses every muscle in your body. I should shoot a workout video, The Seven Minute Seizure. That's probably a good idea.

I turn on my Canon and flick through shots. As I do, I turn the camera away, so she can't see it. She tries to crane her neck, twist her head to see, and I step away.

"I can't let you look at this. Not right now. Not until the world is ready. I hope you understand."

"I understand you have things on there that you don't want a detective to see."

I shrug. She's right. I flick past pictures of corpses and hearts in jars back to Killer Mick inside his fake taxi in the driveway of his home. The moonlight shines on the mailbox showing his address. I turn the viewfinder to her. "This is house you want to go to," I tell her. "This is where you'll find those jars."

She leans in, studies the photo. She flips open a small notebook, jots the number in there. "What street?" she asks.

"I think it is Poplar Street," though I know it is.

"Thanks." She says as she flips the notebook shut and tucks it back into her coat. "Let's say we'll call it an anonymous tip."

"Anonymous is what I'm used to."

She looks at me. "You're a good person for this."

I shake my head. "I'm no person at all."

She nods, lets out a breath, looks down the road, and turns her back to me, marching into the station. Soon, she'll be roaring out in her cruiser with a line of back up, sirens singing a chaotic chorus, lights flashing fireworks. They'll catch a killer, and it'll all be thanks to me.

I'm left to wander down the street, and I wonder what if I gave them my name, maybe that tip wouldn't have been so anonymous, maybe I would have been seen as a hero. Maybe the only thing that's stopping me from being someone important is my habit of being no one at all. I could have been interviewed on the news, remembered not like Charles Manson, but like someone who saves lives, one of those people. Like, who? I can't think of anyone.

I guess no one really remembers heroes.

The sun starts to rise, but the adrenaline and coffee have my skin shaking with jitters of energy, so I keep walking. It's early so there's no one to follow but the streets. That's all right. I hear the sirens before I see the lights. Five cruisers scream past me. I watch them disappear, turning behind a horizon of concrete, while I stroll on. Why did I even help her? Why did I hesitate to help her? I knew a woman who lost her son to a man that murdered him. And I saw how it killed her too.

I turn down Squatter's Row. Under the sunlight no street could ever seem so desolate, so empty, barren. I snap a picture to capture the loneliness.

And then just like my mother, that Detective Silvia will never think of me again.

Moira and her Pal

Tonight, a heat blooms in my stomach, and a thought boils in my brain. A dumb, bad thought. A dangerous, sick wondering thought. I sit in the back of a bar, drinking alone, my usual night. Seated against the wall, I could be some dust-coated painting without a single light to shine over it. I sip and watch the men try to catch women. Men with pickup lines, men offering drinks, men getting nowhere. Me, I'm feeling reckless. I'm feeling restless. My mind shrieks for sleep, but my eyes hold wide. I couldn't sleep if I wanted to, and I know that I don't want to.

I'm thinking that tonight I might talk to someone.

Waiting so long, watching all these people, all these figures, play their parts, wondering when is it gong to be my turn? When do I get to stop spectating? When do I get to step through the glass and join them in the display? I'm sick of waiting.

There's a woman at the bar, a woman I'd follow out of this place at the skip of one of those hearts in a jar. She has hair like syrup folded into a bun over her neck. She sips something alone, glancing around, as she swirls her drink. I stand from my table and stare across the room at her. She doesn't see me. I'm used to it, and it's good. It gives me time to put my thoughts together. I try a strut towards her, but my arms feel stiff, and my body jittery. I start to sweat thinking about how many people die alone on the streets every single night. I could die alone too. Unless I grab a stranger's hand while I slash my own throat, I likely will. Hopefully I'd at least be able to break into someone's house before I die, that way I could die in someone's home. That would be close enough. But tonight I feel like maybe I want more. Maybe I want to try and impress this girl.

Failing to strut, I decide instead to simply saunter over to her, trying to capture a confident sway in my hips. I don't know if I get it right; it's my first time trying to move in a what that I hope to be noticed. No one looks up, though, no surprise there. I'm not an eye-catching man after all.

Sweat soaks through to my skin, pooling in my clothes. How sexy am I? I'm sure she'll love me, a jittery wild eyed man with sweat pouring out of every pore on his skin. Who wouldn't want that? I stand behind her stool. She doesn't turn around or look back. Then I stand behind the empty chair next to her. She sips her drink and stares ahead. I don't know if she doesn't see me or if she's ignoring me. Either one would make sense. I sit down anyway.

The chair shakes as my body touches it, its wood scratching on the floor. I rub my palms together. I try to breathe. I want to breathe. Why can't I breathe? I knock on the top of the bar, because I don't know what else to do, and with this, she finally looks at me. She raises an eyebrow, waiting for a word.

"Hey," I say. That's really all the conversation I know.

She looks me up and down. "You Stew?"

I close my lips, my mind working. I decide to nod. "Yes that's me, I'm Stew."

She sucks on her drink, points an elegant fingernail at it.

"I've had three of these. Do you think it's right to make a woman drink alone?" Her tone is harsh as steel wool.

I shiver in my seat, I'm not sure if I want to be Stew, that might have been a mistake.

"Sorry," I mutter.

"You going to make me pay for them?"

"Absolutely not." I hold myself on one elbow, trying to play at a kind of posture, a tone, of a man who people notice would have. I think of myself as a broad-shouldered man telling stories about saving the lives of African children. I pull out my silver snakeskin wallet and flip it open to an array of cards. I remove one with Platinum written across its face and set it on the counter. These are all things that are definitely mine and belong to me and won't be flagged the second they're used. I hope I can get her out of here quick, but I want to be cool.

"Drink as much as you want. "I say to her.

She raises an eyebrow. "You want me drunk?"

I lean forward and say words that definitely don't belong in my mouth. "I want you however I can get you."

"You already have me," she says with a smile.

I lean close enough to smell the honey in her hair.

"Let's go back to your place then."

"Sounds like a plan."

And with that I pay for her three drinks, and we're gone.

I wonder who Stew is, where Stew is. Why was she waiting for him? This should be the reason to give up every ghost of an idea I had about her and make a break for it, but I guess a mixture of horniness and loneliness is pushing bad ideas into the epicenter of my brain. It can read my fear and panic as a rush, and so I start to enjoy playing a character. I can be anyone. Anyone as long as that person answers to Stew, or Stu, or Stuart.

She walks with me down the sidewalk, stepping beside me. It makes me want to try to hold her hand, but I'm not sure if that's something Stew would do. He feels too cool for that. Maybe he's an arm-in-arm kind of guy. But I don't know how to hook my arm through hers, so I just settle for the casual stroll through the dark that the two of us share.

"What's your name?" I ask.

"Moira," she tells me.

I smile. I can't believe I have a woman's real name, not one that I made up.

"That isn't my real name, of course," she goes on. The stars fall from my eyes, but it'll be okay. She's still a real woman, and even with a fake name that's good enough for me. Oh, god, I suddenly realize, I hope she's a real woman. You can never be sure nowadays.

She shrugs, and goes on, "Just like I'm sure your real name isn't Stew."

Well, she has me there.

We turn a corner to a row of rundown shops with blocks of empty space running between them. We must have been walking at least a mile by now. I look over the smooth curves of her hips and her ass, at her legs that peak from under the hem of her black dress. Urban Outfitters with a deep V front, playing on the curves of her form and only straps for a back. She notices me watching her and lets one of her straps drop a bit. She flashes wanting eyes at me, eyes that I have a dozen pictures of but that I have never seen looking towards me. The excitement of it all rushes the air out of my stomach. If I had my camera, if I could take a picture or two, just to capture her, just to keep her in my camera's memory. My hands move to fondle for the zippers on my camera bag, but I stop them. I don't need to photograph this one. This new sensation makes my fingers tingle, and my heart feel light.

I lift my hand, and I run it over her shoulder. She sighs through her lips, rolls her neck. My fingertips glide down the open back of her dress, sliding on the heat of her skin. I find the small of her back and rub it. She lets the air out of her mouth, and my hands find her ass.

"You like that?" she asks.

My breath runs short, but I push the words out, "I like everything on you."

"Now, Imagine having everything in me."

I know I've had this fantasy before, many times, but fantasies don't ever play out in real life the way you want them to. One time I tried to live my dream of being the comic and cartoon super hero Power Dude, Defender of Rightitude. I punched a neighbor bully in the face. He spat up three teeth, and my mom made me sleep in the back yard for a week.

"You're not at all the way I imagined you," Moira tells me.

We walk off the sidewalk and down a lot toward some window-shattered and long abandoned car dealership. We're out of the city, now, closer to the interstate. More stars show up above. The street is wide but quiet this late at night. Behind the dealerships a hill slopes down to black where I can only make out a thicket of unkempt jagged bushes. She draws my attention from the scene with the tip of her finger.

"You listening?"

"Sure," I say.

"You said you were short and bald. You know you're neither of those things, right?"

I try a smile with a shrug. "Well, I wanted to lower your expectations. You know, give you a surprise."

"Well, I was more surprised by how late you were. I was about to get ready to do this with anyone." She waves a hand toward the old Plymouth building. "This is it."

Weights of fear drop into my shoes and hold my feet fast to the ground. I clear my throat.

"Wouldn't you rather a hotel or something."

She moves a hand forward. "We've got mats and everything set up in here. It's nice. It's remote. You'll like it. Come on."

She sways her hips and crosses the wide avenue toward the rundown building.

Oh, Stew, what have you gotten yourself into this time?

Moira looks over her shoulder in a way that strikes my heart and dick in an equal way, and my shoes lighten. I start to walk after her.

Inside the dealership, blue gym-room mats velcroed together cover the floor like a setup for wrestling practice. Pillows and blankets lie on either side to suggest some semblance of comfort. A few lit candles line the walls of the area, throwing the only light. Moira struts ahead of me. She looks around, peering into the darkness beyond.

"Hey, you still here?" She bends her head side-to-side, afraid to step out into the darkness. "Shit," she hisses, then calls, "You didn't fall asleep, did you?" She looks back, frowns a bit. "Everyone's making me wait tonight, I guess."

"I'm here," a voice formed in the back of a dump truck full of gravel rumbles. "Goddamn, what took you two so long?"

"Stew was late."

Shadows change angles in the dark. The outline of a figure lumbers in the black. Someone who is tall and broad is there. He rubs his belly, thick enough to show in the dark, and stretches out his broadsword arms. He stalks into the light. A man attached to the body of a stone golem, ass naked and ready for action. He holds a pair of dull eyes on me. "You needed to be on time."

"Sorry," I murmur, trying not to look directly at him.

Moira drops her dress. Her white skin shimmers in the candlelight. Her breasts pert and perfect stand full with dark brown nipples. She runs her fingers through her dark peach fuzz down her smooth stomach to her unshaved area below. I start to sweat. She is gorgeous. She looks to me, raising an eyebrow, and I know that she's wondering about my clothing.

I look from one to the other, down at myself. One of us definitely doesn't belong, I think to myself.

"Who's he?" I ask, though I'm sure he's not the delivery man.

"I'm her pal." His voice runs as flat as an earthquake.

"What does it matter who he is?" Moira asks. "You knew there'd be another guy here."

"I know that, but." My voice stops and falls. My eyes drop. I look at all the dirty clothes that hang off my skin. I can bring myself to fantasize about a lot of things, but this just isn't working in my head. I try to see myself naked with them. I know Stew would be naked with them. I swallow and start to work at the button on my jeans while forgetting myself and remembering that tonight I'm Stew. Oh, that Stew, always getting into threeways in abandoned car dealerships with men twice his size. He's such a card, that Stew. I drop my pants and step out of them.

Pal sighs. "Jesus, man. Take your fucking time."

"It is getting late." Moira holds her arms crossed over her chest, covering her nipples. They both stare at me, watching me. I don't like this. I don't think I can do this. I look to the shadowed corners of this abandoned place, and I think of crouching in them. I think of stepping back into the wall. They would never find me if I did. The thought eases me. But I'm not that person right now. Tonight, I'm Stew, and Stew would undress in front of anyone. All you need to do is ask, and he'll deliver the goods.

But I can't. My fingers hold the waist to my boxers, and they just won't let them drop. My fingers unfurl as the breath leaves my chest. I want to grab this woman's hips and fuck her senseless with this guy watching on and then high five him after we finish. I know it happens. I've seen it online. But it just doesn't happen for me.

"I'm sorry," I start.

But Pal cuts me off. "Oh, you fucking son of a bitch! What? Did you just come here to laugh at us? Is this some bullshit joke to you?"

"No, I just." I lift a hand. "I think I've made a mistake. I'm just not comfortable with this."

"Pull out your fucking dick," Pal roars.

"No."

He lunges a step before I can think to lift a hand, and he hits me. The knuckles of his fist pack hard against my face. His bones are evidently stronger than mine, because I feel my cheek shatter. I never did drink much milk.

I fall onto the ground and cry out, trying to cover my face. Then this naked gorilla straddles me and slams his fists into my nose, one after another. That shatters too, and a mixture of blood and snot slicks up my lips. I open my mouth to scream, while Moira just opens her arms wide and shakes her head in that nothing-I-can-do-here-buddy sort of way. In the meantime her pal sends another cracking blow into the side of my face. He grabs my hair and slams the back of my head against the concrete floor of the dealership entrance. If only we made it to the mats. The second time he slams my head down, I feel the blood pool from my split scalp and stick in my hair. I gasp as he drives an elbow into my neck. He punches the other side of my face, letting my hair go.

My head drops to the floor, and I watch the blood stream from the inside of my mouth, where he split my cheek, and across the floor toward Moira. Her pal stands up and kicks my side, driving the bold bones of his toes into my kidney. I'd cry and cough, but my throat won't work, and my lips are stuck together with blood. Pal grips a new fistful of my bloody hair, and he drags me across the ground and out through the doors into the fresh air and starlight.

I can only half-see the sky, because one of my eyes has welded shut with blood and is swelling. His grip on my hair feels like he's uprooting my scalp. The pain in my face pulses in spiking throbs that make my eyes roll back. Pal drags me to the edge of dealership, to the hill out back, my arms hanging over the side.

He delivers another first-class express boot to my kidney, and I roll over the edge. I topple down the slope, and my body finds the thorn bushes at the bottom. The tiny hooks shred through my naked legs, drawing blood and sticking inside when the momentum of my rolling body tears them free. More thorns latch into my neck and arms. A few find some remaining flesh on my face to rip away as they create a crown of thorn boughs around my head. I cough blood and groan silently in the dark. My hands slap for the ground and I find it under me. I roll myself away from the thorns to where no new pain can tear into me, only the steady throb from the tip of my skull down into the bottom of my calves.

"I think I killed him," I hear pal's voice shout as he saunters back into the dealership.

Nope. Joke's on him. I'm still pretty much alive.

I feel for my blood-stained shirt, and the broken body parts I'm not too afraid to touch. I can't breathe through my nose and barely through my mouth. My fingers grip the grass, and I realize all my camera bags are still in the dealership. Shit. All my faces, all my voices, all my nights. All sitting there with my discarded pants on that bloody floor. It's some expensive shit. They might take it. They could sell it. I can feel new endorphins spilling into my system. I can't let them do that. I can't let them take that from me. I need those. I need those memories. I can't go without them. My mind races with worry, with thoughts of the morning and an empty bag, of starting over again. I can't do that. I'll kill myself if they do that. I need to get them.

My red hands twist into the ground, grabbing clumps of grass, and my torn legs shove me up the hill. Through busted lips and a broken mouth I can hear little grunts fall out of me. I drag myself up that hill, feeling only every shriek of pain in the back of my head. There will be plenty of time to breakdown later. Right now, I need to save my shit.

I drag myself to the top of the hill, just feet away from the edge of the dealership lot. I can see Moira standing under the moonlight, her dress half-on. She is talking to someone so that I have to turn my head to see who with my one good eye. He's short, fat, bald, and in glasses. He waves his hands about, jabbering at her. She watches him, listening like a painting would listen to a dining room's conversation. Indifferent but there. When she responds, they're with the curt phrases she always uses.

That man must be Stew. He looks out of breath. Did he follow us? Without my equipment I can't hear a word they are saying, but I can imagine it.

Moira drops the straps of her dress, mouthing, "Do you still want to go inside and fuck me in front of a man twice your size?"

Stew grins. "Boy, do I!"

I have a feeling that I'm not too far off this time. She leads him to the entrance. I wait awhile before moving up behind them. With my body in the shape that it is I'm sure I'll drop grunts and hisses as I go, and I can't afford to get caught. I don't need another train to run through me like the last one.

I stalk, being a desecrated thing, a movie monster of a man, around the lot and toward the building's back. I peer through a shattered display window. There's no glass remaining in its opening. Only the black of night stretches on through it. I set my hands on the side of the window frame and carefully step myself up through. I totter half-through the window and hope that there's no glass waiting for me on the inside.

Once inside, I drop down. Not with any elegance save for a leg that barely moves and arms that flash in pain at every twitch. Glass does lay at the bottom of the window. Not from the window but from shards of a dozen beer bottles smashed against the floor. They crunch under me, as I roll through them. More pain flashes into my bones, sending light across my eyes in a place where there is none. You'd think that I would have stopped feeling the pain at some point. But every new ounce of blood I loose comes with new pain. I wonder if this is how Jennifer felt. But she's dead. That's probably worse.

My grunts and the crunching of glass beneath me don't matter here. I can hear the moans bubbling over from the blue mats that overshadow any noise that I'm making. I stand up on legs that twitch and tremble, and I wander forward toward the candle light. As I get close, I fall to my hands and crawl like an animal to make any progress against the straining of every wire and nerve in my frame. I prowl through the broken doorways of the old sales offices until I reach the little light that is coming through this place.

In this glow, the short man sits with his side to me. His head is back, eyes closed. Moira's head is all the way down on him between his thighs. Her tower of pain and misery holds her by the sides and pounds her from behind. Her groans come out muffled, but both of the men add their own sounds. All eyes are on her, none on me.

Just an inch into the light on the far side, my pants and bag lay alongside a long streak of blood from where my head scrapped across the floor and out of this building.

I lean out of the dark, my face and arm blocking the candlelight. My shadow throws across their bodies like the twisted hand and deformed head of a mongoloid freak. But this trio is too caught in their trance to notice me. I'm sure their groans would change, if they did. I wish I had taken their offer; I wish I felt that I was feeling their pleasure instead of this pain. But different things are meant for different people, I guess.

I make it over to my pants, sitting in the shadows, my bag pressed to my chest. It's there that the relief finally hits me, my bones going back to stone, and my muscles tightening to rods. My Adrenaline, which had pushed me this far, flees and leaves the ruins that is me behind. I can barely move my fingers to unzip and check the contents of my bag. But all my equipment seems to still be in there, undisturbed. They haven't been through it. They didn't have the time. They don't know my memories. That makes me happy, but it doesn't stop the flashes of fire in my skull.

I need to ignore it. I need to escape the pain. From the dark I watch their bodies moving together just ahead of me. I see the bloody bruises on Pal's knuckles gripping Moira's hips white. He grimaces and grunts, but he feels no pain. I want to be able to escape like the way they are. My hands start their easy work. They assemble the mic without my thinking. I only pay attention to the three of them, to their moans, to their lust. I turn the mic on and pull up the camera on them.

Their faces contort, and their bodies gyrate. Lines of feverish movement run through every one of my shots, filled with ghosts of sexual thrusts and twists. Grunts and sighs of ecstasy run from their throats, their bodies pounding. Wet slaps ring out from Moira's lower body and slurping cries of pleasure rumble up from her chest. I snap shot after shot, take after take, and I feel like I'm with them. I'm in it with them. I'm all of them. I'm more than just Stew. I'm Pal. I'm Moira. With all this, I could I be alone?

I continue to snap my shots as they build to climax and a final flourish of fluids and cries. And just like I imagine, the two men high five each other. Oh, that Stew, I think. The men grin; Moira pants exhausted. They all lie down as they let their orgasms settle. I pack my bag and pull my shattered body through the carpeted office rooms toward the backmost part of the building. I clear away an area of glass and metal and settle into a corner near an unbroken window, farther back than any of them should need to travel. I rest there as close into the corner as my body can fit. I close my eyes, and sleep finds me. I'm content to be a wall again, tonight.

Walls don't feel pain.

Leon But Worse

Patrolling the daylight with a twisted, mangled body, dried blood oozing from my eye and mouth, more running fresh from the cuts on my legs and arms, does not make for a pretty sight. No matter how much I wanted to slink out of view, pedestrians caught sight of my deformed frame, and grimaced and jerked their faces away as if someone shocked them with electricity in the neck. I don't have any insurance for the hospital. I told a nurse running the front desk that I had a credit card, but she didn't seem to care. I don't understand why. I have money. I'm obviously in a bad state. Why not fix me? But they wouldn't. No one will.

A boy walked up to me, offering me a half-eaten candy bar. Hungry I reached toward it, but his mother wrangled his wrist, pulled him away, before he could mouth a word. What a sad state I must be in when even the charity of children isn't allowed. I stumble, slump and half-sleep in a pile of waste until the hot sun fades and the night takes its reign. Pus bubbles in wounds on my arms, legs, and chest. Flailing in alleys where bodies riddled with disease find a comfortable home is bound to breed infection in any man. Shit. I really didn't plan on dying like this. I wonder how long my body would have to lie between the streets before anyone would find it, grey and cold. I imagine it would be bloating, popping, and decomposing, surrounded by wet filth, until feral dogs would take what was left and gnaw, chew, and swallow me into oblivion. Leave me like Frisky, the feral cat. Like Jennifer, the feral girl. At least I would be in good company as the feral boy.

But what would happen to my camera?

I carry myself to the only home I still have entrance to, the only place I know I can get in, even if I'm not allowed. I've spent so much time on the streets, in the dark, that even with one eye crusted over and bolts of pain distracting my mind from my task, the muscle memory of my legs carry me to the brick tower, to those couple steps that lead to that door. I swipe my card in the card reader and whisper a prayer to whatever degenerate Dog God birthed a place where someone like me could exist.

It answers my prayers and the door clicks open.

Even the Dog God of degenerates can be generous sometimes.

I saunter in, the night only just beginning, bodies marching, perusing, and loitering in the lobby as I pass through. I'm usually a master at disappearing, but tonight the only wallpaper I resemble is the type that guests notice for how distorted with bubbles of leaking water and crusts of mold it looks, how unhealthy it feels just to stand near. All the eyes in the lobby turn, all the faces fall, and everyone wants to be as far away from me as they can get.

I drag myself through their lobby, pus dripping from my wrist and leaving its white trail across their fine carpet. But that's none of my concern. They should be so lucky as to collect pieces of me in the fibers of their building. Remember, I'm going to be someone. They can afford to replace it, anyway. And I'm sure they will.

A doorman in a green suit walks to me with one arm raised. I lift the card, with my room number on it, to his pale face. He stops short of me and looks over the card from his safe distance.

"Where did you find that?" he asks.

I huff as broken a laugh as my torn throat can call.

"It's mine. I live here. I'm Leon."

The doorman waits a moment as he thinks about this. I pull myself toward the elevator. He comes after me, and stands in front of me, opening his arms, keeping to the left so he won't accidentally make contact with me.

"There is no Leon in this building," he informs me.

Shit. Right.

I nod. A line of suits and dresses has formed along the walls, all eyes are on me. I've never seen so many people paying attention to me. Just me. I feel flattered. It's obviously for the wrong reasons, but still. The man at the front desk lifts his phone and punches in some numbers. That can't be a good thing. So, I run and dive just as the elevator doors open. As I lunge, I whip a hand back at the doorman chasing me, and a wad of my pus and blood slaps him in the cheek. He stops dead, feels his face, and looks at his palm, his mouth twisting the way an infant's would when it screams and no one knows why.

The old woman stepping from the elevator yells when she sees me lunging past her. My side hits the elevator floor, and I scramble to my feet. No one on the inside moves to touch me or stop me. They only watch from their frozen positions pushed up in the corners. I slap the button for the top floor and lower myself onto my ass. Breaths drag and drop from my constricted throat. The elevator plays no music, it only buzzes steadily with each floor it passes on its way to the top.

When the doors open, I stand and stumble into the hall, falling against the wall on the far side. I drag my shoulder across it and find Leon's front door. A slip of the same key opens it. Why hasn't he changed his locks? Why hasn't he asked for a new key? Why hasn't he canceled his card? He's had more than enough time, that Leon. Does he really like me that much? Maybe he did have that feeling in the car. Maybe he did want me to be his protégé, his replacement. Does he need a best friend? Well, I've come back. You can teach me more, Leon.

The apartment runs black straight to the bedroom door, where a line of white light peeks out from under the notch. I shut the door behind me, and the sound of the automated lock clicking shut rings through the halls. Leon's bed creaks. His door opens. My body is too stiff, my legs too throbbing with pain, for me to move quickly enough or reliably enough to skulk out of his sight. So, I stand there, and let myself be seen.

The light from his bedroom opens in a bight bar; his body blocking a good deal of the light, but I know he can still see me darkened under his own shadow. He stands there only in jeans, wearing no shirt. His face is haggard, tired, no teeth-baring grin, his chin and cheeks jagged with facial hair. He's still beautiful, but it's a dimmer sort of beauty.

"You," he grunts.

"Me," I agree.

The phone in his living room rings. He flicks on the light, struts towards it. I can't see him past the wall, but I can hear him lift the receiver.

"Hello? Yeah. Yeah, there's a guy in here. No, it won't be a problem. Thanks. All right. No, no, don't do that. He'll be fine. Sorry. Of course I'll pay for the carpet. You can charge that to me. It's all right. Thank you. Thanks. Bye."

The phone clicks back into its cradle. Leon paces back into the hallway. He glances at me. His face doesn't change like the others' did. He paces into the kitchen. He clicks that light to white as well. He clears his throat.

"Come on in. Sit down."

I hobble into his kitchen. A slight scent curls in my battered nose. It's not much, and the table, sink, floor, walls, and counters all run as spotless and shimmering as I remember. But that smell lingers, something festering and rotten, like meat forgotten in the garbage disposal that molds and attracts flies, who lay their eggs in it that become maggots. Leon pulls out a chair for me. I let myself fall into it. He walks away, strutting into the hallway and disappearing toward his bedroom.

My single good eye turns and looks out toward his window. A single slate of plywood boards the hole where I shattered it, where the woman climbed out and fell to her death, when Leon couldn't save her. I remember how I felt walking away from that disaster that he couldn't fix. I felt so good. I felt almost superhuman. Now, I'm even less than the less-than-human I was before.

Leon enters and sets spools, bandages and needles on the kitchen table. He sets down bottles of alcohol and peroxide, and tubes of creams, as well. Of course, this magic man is a field doctor, a hero, a savior, and I'm sure a mean fuck. Why does one person get so much? I can't help but wonder if his having so much is part of the reason why I have so little.

"You don't look so good," he tells me as he readies his needle and thread. His voice running as empty as a car coasting down a hill.

"I could say the same to you," I cough.

"No you couldn't. Not the same."

He leans in with the needle in his hand and splashes my face with alcohol. I cough and cry out, as he digs the point of the needle through the flesh above my eye. He drags it through my brow, pushes it back in, and pulls it through again. I hiss and twitch against him, but my muscles are tired from dragging my countless infections around, so I don't have it in me to fight.

He finishes with my eye and snips the line. "I figured it was you who broke in that night. You stole from me. You know you're the only person who has ever stolen from me."

I feel that I might be grinning at him, but my face muscles don't respond the way they should.

"That was me. You have no idea how it felt climbing all the way up here. It was terrifying but in an amazing way."

"You know that break in cost a girl her life."

"A girl you couldn't save."

I call out a hoarse moan as he splashes more alcohol on my arm. He adds peroxide, and it bubbles, as he picks pebbles out from my wound. Then he starts to sew.

"Why did you leave me your stuff?" I ask him. "Why not change it over?"

His eyes focus on his work.

"I thought maybe you needed it more than I did. I also thought that maybe you'd come back."

"Why would you want me back?"

He shrugs, splashes more alcohol onto my chest, It runs down and burns my legs as well causing my mind to reel in pain. I pant, gasp and tremble in my chair. He sews at my chest without a glance at my pained face.

"I was good to you," he goes on. "Why would you steal from me? I just don't understand. I'm a good person. I would have given to you. So, why steal?"

My head lulls against the bolts of pain sparking through my skull. When he's finished sewing, he rubs creams over my wounds. "No reason. I just wanted to. I wanted to have you."

"To have me?"

"To have what you have. To be you."

His needle digs into a muscle on my leg, and I scream. My eyes flash to his face, and, for a moment, I think I see him grin. He must like this; he must enjoy torturing me. He knows that I stole part of him that night. And now he wants revenge, but he's too polite to call it that. He finishes my leg and wraps a white wrap of bandages around it.

"I've never seen anyone die before," he tells me. "Especially not someone so close to my hands."

My head falls forward, and my neck feels too weak to lift it back up.

"I took pictures," I grunt.

I feel him shudder when his needle touches my arm. He cuts into my skin, but he doesn't stop there, even though I feel the fresh red bubble of blood rise up from the pinprick.

"Why?" his voice rumbles.

"I have pictures of everything. I'm really good at it. They are actually quite tasteful."

He treats and wraps the last of my cuts in silence. He puts his bottles, creams, needles and stitches together and carries them back down the hall and into his bedroom, out of sight. He's gone for a while, and when he comes back he's holding a bottle of whiskey. He sets it on the table between us and fishes through the cabinets for two tumblers. The china and the glasses are no longer ordered, no longer pristine or even stacked. Everything hidden behind those doors is in disarray, a silent disorder. Eventually he finds two glasses, though, and sets one in front of me. Tiny flecks of dust have gathered on its bottom. But I have so much bad shit in my blood right now, how can I begrudge a couple smudges? Leon pours into my glass.

"For the pain."

I nod. My fingers wrap the glass, but lifting it takes effort. The fresh pain of his needle and the soreness of the day have broken me. He helps the glass reach my lips, and the flood of whiskey numbs them and my tongue and my throat, and it warms my stomach in a steaming splash that radiates into my bones. I sigh in exhilaration and let the glass drop onto the table.

"I could be you," I let him know through my hoarse throat. "I could. It's easy to be you. You know I have some of you now, so you get it. I was almost in a threeway last night." I lift a hand to him, squeezing my fingers together so that only a thin opening peeks through. "This close," I tell him. "This close."

"Good for you." He says as he pours me another glass.

I lift the glass to my lips more quickly than I should. My hand shudders, and a splash of the gold liquid smacks the top of the table. Seeing this, Leon stands and turns his back to me. Look at those muscles, I marvel. Round, hard. Even on his back they're big enough to cast shadows over his body. A perfect line runs down his spine to the nape of his back where it connects to a similarly heavenly shaped ass. He pulls a paper towel from the roll and wipes up my spill. I let the whiskey drain down my throat and cascade into my stomach, throwing more warmth and numbing drunkenness into my frame. My head wobbles, feeling like it's not attached to me but in a good way.

"You've lost it," I go on. The steam from the alcohol churns in my stomach and rises up my throat. "You've lost it, and I've found it. Look at you. Where are your women? Huh? Who were you fucking tonight? No one but yourself, that's who."

He pours me another tumbler, not touching his own. I slam it down, splashing most of the sticky sweetness on my chin. We hold eyes. His dull and resigned, mine burning like a fire trapped in stone, my stomach swelling with smoke.

"You let her die," I rant on. "You let her die, and you lost yourself. You let me win, and I got you. You know I did. You wanted me to come back; and you know why? Because you wanted to see the man who took your perfection away. You're so sexy, so fucking smart, so cool. Made of plastic. A fucking model. I've seen your kind everywhere. TV screens, store displays, magazines. You think you can just have it all? Don't you?"

He pours me another glass. I throw it somewhere near my face, though I have no idea how much actually gets into my mouth. The fire in my stomach spreads into my muscles and throat.

"You've lost your soul. You've lost your throne. I have it. I even have your soul. You gave it to me. Just fucking gave it to me."

I try to stand, but I can't feel my legs, and I fall backward. My body bucks onto the chair, and it topples over. I hit the ground. Leon stands from his side of the table.

"I made you a bed on the couch," his voice rumbles. "You can rest there. Leave in the morning. Don't do too much or your stitches will split."

I can only lie and watch the thick, rugged feet of the man I want to be walk away from me.

I don't sleep. How can I? This man, this testament of perfection lies only feet away in his bed. He's let me into his sanctuary. He doesn't understand what he's done. He's letting himself slip. Now, I can be him. I can be perfect, I can be noticed, I can be loved. I don't have to be stared at only when I'm too disgusting to be ignored. I can want to be wanted.

I pace through his kitchen. My muscles throbbing blasts of pain, but I'm used to it. I find that I can function against each jolt, using the electricity in my bones. I pull his drawers open one by one and fish through the silverware. One window still shines in with moonlight. In a drawer I find something that sets my blood cold, though my heart pounds faster. I hold the heavy black handle and lift it toward me. Its long silver blade reflects my stitched and wrapped face. I swing the knife, and it slices the air effortlessly with a whipping sound from a kung fu flick. It feels strong, sturdy in my grip. I shut the drawer and carry it with me.

I stalk down the hallway, my head feeling light like it's following behind the rest of me. I can almost see the back of my own body pacing forward, making its steady way toward the bedroom door of this man who stands for everything I could never be, not as long as he exists. But if he doesn't exist, then doesn't someone have to replace him?

His golden knob turns, and his door opens without a sound. Thin moonlight throws grey through his bedroom. It smells like dust and cigarettes. What a filthy habit for such a clean man. Clothes litter the floor. The bathroom door stands open. I see myself reflected in his vanity, gripping his knife and looking as placid as a sleepwalker. My head burns. I'm sick. I'm tired. I'm drunk. I need to sleep. I know this; I used to know when enough is enough. But my body keeps moving. I want my feet to stop. Don't I?

As I stand beside Leon's bed, my fingers wrap into his covers. They feel like silk but smell like stale sweat. There's a blankets bundle just under his neck. I pull them back and reveal the top of his chest, that collar bone that runs like a club under his skin. His pecks sculpted in the lines you only see on comic book super heroes, the same for his stomach. I flip the covers off his body, and I see that he sleeps in the nude. No inch of him disappoints. Looking over his full figure I only feel disappointed with myself. How can I be so far from him and yet so close to him? I need to be closer. I need to be him.

I need to put down the knife and leave. I know better than what I'm about to do. My mother taught me better than this. Maybe not better than stalking. Maybe not better than hiding. Maybe not better than breaking in. Maybe not better than reveling in people's misery. But she certainly taught me better than murder.

I remember when she lifted a stolen revolver to my dad's face that night when I wished I could have been anywhere else, anyone else. He gripped the barrel of the gun, screamed for her to shoot, then tore the revolver from her hand and turned it on her. He fired, and the bullet sunk through her stomach but didn't come out the other side. It didn't kill her, only my brother who was only two months away from being born.

I remember that she smiled when my old man went to prison, but she cried every night following. Nights that made me want to run, want to find somewhere better to be, someone better to be.

Still lost in this thought, I see Leon's eyes snap open and peer into me. His mouth drops as shivers wrack through my bones. I use that tremor of anxious energy to do something awful. My arm raises the blade up and throws it down before Leon can even breathe.

Blood runs over his perfect skin, pools into the wells where the muscles of his chest meet. Leon grips the handle of the blade in both hands. He sucks a strained breath and lets it whisper free from his throat. I stand and watch, frozen to the base of my spine. My mind still tries to work some kind of understanding out of what I've done, trying to process the memory like a stomach would with swallowed stones. I don't get it. I can't figure it out, so I fumble through my bag, and I pull out my camera, snapping pictures of Leon wrestling with the knife.

He pulls the blade out of his chest. He gasps and sighs. His fists tremble. His fingers twitch and let go of the handle. His head falls back. He sighs and breathes, sighs and breathes. His throat hitches, and he cries out.

"Why?" he whines.

Sweat streaks down his forehead. Tears well on his eyes and break down his cheeks. I can't believe I'm seeing someone so cool, so perfect, at such a low. I snap more photos of his face while he cries and tries reaching his blood-streaked and shaking hands toward me.

"Why?" he repeats. "Why?"

I lower the camera, look into his eyes of pure pain. And I know for certain that no one else has ever seen him like this.

"Because you exist," is all I can think to say.

I grip the hilt of his knife and wrench it from his body. He lets another moan break from his throat. I think of my mom with that gun and what my dad did when she was too afraid to pull the trigger, and I let the blade fall into him again. Leon cries out. I pull the blade up, the revolver fire flashing in my mind, and I sink it back in. I pull it out. My mother screams. I slam it back in. She grips her stomach. I pull it out. Blood paints her hands. I slam it back in. She screams again. I pull it out. My dad drops the gun. I slam it back in. He tells me to get him a beer. I pull it out. And he kicks me to get my ass moving. I slam it back in.

There's so much blood I don't know what to do. Leon's stopped crying like my mom did for a while. I had to drag my mother across the street in the middle of the night to a neighbor's house while my dad slept, so they could call an ambulance. I didn't know the number.

My fingers tremble on his shoulders like they did on my mother's. I pull him from the bed, dragging him into the bathroom.

"I'm sorry. I'm so sorry," I whisper in shaking breaths.

I pull him up and let his body slide and slump into the bathtub. My palms are dripping red. I think of my mother's and my brother's blood pooling onto my fists as I held a balled towel against her stomach in the neighbor's kitchen. She was so white. Leon's skin is turning that same shade of white.

I open his cabinet, grab the tools he used to fix me. I don't know what else to do. I don't know how to think, or how to feel. I feel like I'm a kid again tonight. I'm growing up too much, too fast, and I want it to stop.

I know I've seen the dead, but I can't have killed someone. I can't be responsible for his death. I just can't be responsible.

I splash his body with the same alcohol that he did mine. I pour peroxide over him. I slip the needle through one of the knife wounds disfiguring his chest and neck, but I can't get the thread to pull through after it. My fingers are shaking too much. I let the needle and thread fall to the bottom of the tub, and I sit beside him, screaming, and crying.

But he's staying dead. I know he's dead. I'm not that stupid. This man is dead, and I know I killed him.

So, I lift my camera to my eyes, and I snap pictures of this perfect man's ruined corpse. Some with the lights on, some with the lights off. I try different angles for different drama. Some look like crime scene photos. Some are intimate enough to almost be pornographic. I may have ruined his life, but I will not ruin his beauty. I commit to him forever inside my lens. When I'm finished taking his pictures, I pull myself away. I'm no longer a child. I'm a man now. And now that this man is dead, I know which man I want to be. I can become him.

His clothes—Versace, Armani, Pierre Balmain— are still too big for me, but I use his Salvatore Ferragamo belts to tighten, and I roll them up to fit my legs and arms. I make them work. Even if his head is bigger than mine, and his hats fall over my eyes, and he's too large for me to fill, I'll make it work. I'll grow into them. I shut the bathroom door. In the bedroom I think I can hear him whimper. I think I hear him crying. But I know he's dead. And so I go into the living room, but I still think I can hear him. When I get to the kitchen, I pour myself a drink. He's still crying like my mom did when she felt her stomach for the son she'd never have, the son I'd never be able to replace. But I can replace Leon. I have already started to.

Dressed, I leave my apartment and take my elevator down to the lobby floor. Despite the late hour, the doorman stands at the end of the carpet.

"Watch your step," he calls to me when the elevator opens. "We had a bit of a biohazard spill from a trespasser earlier in the evening."

I nod.

"Hitting the town late tonight, sir?"

"Just getting some air."

He opens the door for me, and I leave my building and enter the fresh quiet of the dark. And as I leave my home behind I don't hear my mother cry; I don't feel my uselessness. I feel that I am free to go anywhere. I feel that I am free to become anyone. I am anyone. Not me, not Stew, not Leon. Something more, something amazing, something unimaginable just hours ago. I walk on, until when I look back I won't be able to find my way to home again. Until even when mom calls the cops on me they won't be able to find me. I won't ever go back. I'm free, and I never have to be myself again.

Shit Beetle

Every no-talent asshole dreams of fame, fortune, naked bodies splayed across the ground for them to pick and choose. Everyone dreams of being more than they have any right to be. But no one—not a soul, not a mind, not an exhale of sour breath—puts the effort toward becoming more. Those who truly rise above do so by forcing their way through. Now, I've forced my way through; I've dragged myself up. I've had blood on my hands and sweat in my hair. But no longer. I stalk in elegance. Eyes turn to me. They see my clothing, a flash of the pearls in my mouth, and they melt. I strut through the ooze of their liquid admiration. And I have earned that.

But sometimes a worthless fuckface of a nobody gets a crowd to spill into an art gallery on a Friday night, because no one knows any better, and they don't understand that what they see isn't art—it's piss, breast milk, blood, and semen mixed into something only half-resembling true talent. But no one cares, anymore. If someone says you're an artist, then that's all it takes. No argument, no questions asked. What a load of shit.

Such a crowd spills into the street ahead of me tonight, all suits and cocktail dresses, a few hip souls clad in denim and shredded cotton, clamoring around the enormous door of the perpetual 'it' gallery, bathed in white, peering toward the frames on the walls, primed to see whatever abortion this hackjob has on display this year. They murmur and fidget while they wait, their voices striking the same chords as clusters of flies on a corpse. There's never been a time I wished more for a speeding car to blast down the road out of control and smear blood, bone, and skin for a block before coming to a stop. I would photograph that, make something real, something visceral, something that's meant to be seen, something that can't be ignored. Not like this jerkoff with his plastic cross dropped into his own piss.

But that's not how tonight goes, even though I earned it. Even though Leon is dead, and even though I now stand the ultimate Alpha, somehow the powers that be have set some cockroach of a man into the gallery where I should be receiving endless adoration and praise.

"I hear his photographs capture the human soul," one asshole chirps above the general buzz.

"True human suffering," another goes on. "True human nature."

More like true human shit.

The doors open, and the crowd pushes in. I putter behind them, waiting to see what shit this insect has rolled into art. One of those Shit Beetles. That's all he is, just feeding off shit, swallowing it down, filling up on fecal matter, and shitting it back out to us in these glowing white walled rooms. I haven't seen him or heard him, but his soul radiates that title. Shit Beetle. What else could suit him?

The group totters into the white light, to a middle-aged gallerist with a sharp face, tight lips, and red-stained hair shaking hands and welcoming patrons to witness "the photography that will embody the twenty-first century." Each new body to enter gazes in wonder for a moment, before strolling to some corner or cluster to chat and gawk at stills that I can't discern from any angle.

When I was a boy walking by my mother's side, before my dad wrenched a pistol from her hands and before the brother I never knew died in my mother's stomach, I would cross by this gallery almost every day. It's stood for art since the early nineteen nineties, a testament to time and a landmark in an ever-changing cityscape. I shot pictures of those windows, of the crowds gathered inside and of the workmen setting sculptures and portraits for a night's show. I figured one day those men would set my photos on the wall, that I would gather an audience, that I would be the eyes of my generation. There was a time when that might have been more than I am, but I've waded through filth, I've followed desolate souls to every corner of this shit-streaked city. I've grown into suits and shoes I was never meant to wear. I've become a different man. I've become someone who deserves to be recognized for his dream. And I can't help but let a hate well in my chest as the crowd opens for me, and I step into the white glow of the gallery showroom.

A cold claw grips my hand.

"Good evening, sir," this spike-faced woman greets me. She closes her other hand over my knuckles like she's afraid I'll try to escape. "And welcome to an exhibition of photographs that will change the way you see humanity."

Fat chance.

"I do hope you'll take a chance to purchase a piece for yourself, before they become priceless rarities, naturally."

I turn on my heels to see what sort of art could capture the soul, could steal my imagination with such profound plunderings of the human soul as this woman is shilling, and my eyes fall on a series of photographs gracing the side wall of the cavernous building. My heart skips. My mouth opens. My stomach twists like a noose around a neck. I grip my bag.

"How?" my throat hitches. "How did you?"

In the series, my eyes focus in on a photo of a woman sitting in a red car with a man. Neither one looks at each other. Others show the two out of the car, standing on opposite sides blowing the smoke of the cold night air. Another shows them sitting on the hood. Another captures their desperate kiss. From the speakers in the ceiling you can hear them talking. More pictures show a woman wandering the street alone. Another set within the series plays a slideshow of her and a priest talking, kissing, groping, and him carting her off and pulling her into his Church-like castle. And in the outer and bottom rim of this set a corpse lies on the ground, torn, eaten, destroyed, and desolate. All the beauty gone, and only the misery of her soul left behind.

This is how my Jennifer was meant to be seen. But this isn't how she was meant to be shown.

I twist my neck, stare through the crowd to where the spike-nosed woman leads a cluster of suited fuckers to where our Shit Beetle stands perched. But it's no man, it's a bald woman, black, in a crimson and black dress. She's young, mid-twenties, maybe. She beams and opens her lips that match her dress, showing the rows of white teeth stacked in her mouth. She grins. Her green eyes flash. She stands before a giant wall-sized print of a burning man. I can't hear what she's saying over the buzz of the crowd, but I can gather the gist of her speech.

"Oh, yeah, thank you, they are great. There's a man out there with true talent and skill, a man who's skills outpace any photographer or human being, a man who deserves all your recognition and praise, but these aren't his photographs, they are mine. I stole all of this from him. I cheated him out of his livelihood, and I hope he drowned in the shit I've pushed out and onto his face."

She throws her head back and laughs here, like a bitch.

Pictures of streets, buildings, birds, even a Polaroid of my own mother stands against a wall that reads, "Early Work." Who is this woman? How did she invade my life? Had she been following me since I was a boy? Has she been steadily stealing every piece of art I've created? Did she know how important I was to become? She must have. And I never saw it. She's been following and stealing from me my whole life, and I never saw it.

The realization twists my stomach. My head rolls over itself. I stumble past a pair of suits and lean my shoulder against a wall where a cluster of photographs that depict a cabbie butchering corpses stands.

"Excuse me," the bird woman's voice breaks through the clatter of chit chat.

"Excuse me, but you can't seriously lean against any of these photos. If you dent or scratch the frames, you are purchasing them. No exceptions."

The woman pulls me by the arm. She tries to tug me away from these glorious forgeries. These aren't the originals. I have the originals. Fuck her. She doesn't even know what she's talking about. She's been cheated by the little Miss Shit Beetle over there like I've been cheated. She doesn't know what's happening. My stomach lurches. My hands grip my midsection, and I heave toward the middle of the floor.

Hot orange floods from my throat, splattering on the ground. It splashes the white tile and floods towards the circle of polished shoes and expensive pants. Clusters shout and prance away like TV housewives at the sight of mice.

I wipe my mouth on my sleeve. It doesn't matter; I now have eight coats like it at home.

"My god," the bird face squawks. "You need to leave! You need to leave, now!"

"These are mine," I grumble to her. My tongue feels slow and my throat unsure.

"These are all mine. I shot these. This is my whole life. She followed me my whole life. She followed me. She didn't taken any of these. These pictures are mine! Mine! You Shit Beetle! You!"

I jab a finger in the air toward the bald woman who stole my dreams. She watches me with wide eyes that shake, the eyes of a woman who knows she's been caught. I might as well have found her on top of another man. She knows what she did, and it's going to tear her soul apart.

"You know you did it! You know you stole these pictures!" I shout to her.

A pair of police officers cross through the front doors. Without a moment's warning they grab my shoulders. They speak slowly into my ear, call me sir, and force my heels through my own vomit to drag me away. I don't fight, but I point, and I shout, and I bark all the fury my soul can muster.

"You little black cunt! You dirty, thieving bitch! You stole my work, you stole my life from me! These are my memories! These are mine! You followed me! You've been stalking me, you cunt licking shit fuck! You sick bitch! You've been following me! You've been—"

This is where my voice cuts off, because I start to cry.

I fall to my knees on the sidewalk outside, gasping a breath down, and start to sob. I swallow and can taste my vomit, and I sob some more. The two officers just stand over me. As the doors to the gallery shut behind me, I hear the bird bitch click her tongue against her teeth and prattle, "This city really needs to do more about its homeless."

"I live in a penthouse, you fucking cunt. And I killed for it. What did you ever do for your life?"

"Are you okay?" one of the officers asks over me. "Have you been drinking? Do we need to take you to the hospital?"

I need to run. I need to leave. I can't let the police take me. If they take me to jail, someone might recognize me. They might wonder where I got my clothes from. They might find my key-card, my credit cards. They might look into it while I sit behind bars. They won't understand what I've done. Silvia will have another killer to bring to justice. And this time it will be me.

I try to stand, but my legs quake and I let out a shaking breath.

"No, I'm all right." I look the officer in the eyes. A hitch catches in my throat as I lurch forward, and both the officers jump out of my way. And then I weave toward the middle of the street and dash away.

My fists pump; my over large shoes slap the sidewalk. My breathing drags too ragged and heavy for me to hear if they're following me. But I run, and I run, and I don't look back. Because if I do, I might catch a glimpse of my memories hung by another person on a gallery's famous wall.

A figure weaves ahead, catching my eye. I hold my breath. Has one of the cops doubled around to catch me? A spot of blonde shows in the streetlight, then a flash of an eye. A girl's face shines in the shadow. It's Cinderella, and it's long after midnight. Her face stretches along the jaw and cheek bones, her eyes fall into her face, and her front teeth peek out from under her lips when she turns her face to me. She nudges her head toward an alley, head dissolving into shadow. Does she want me to follow? My aching legs stomp after her.

Her hair flashes even in the claustrophobic dark of the alleyway. I follow her out into the streets, where the lights throw white across the pitch black pavement. She shows her back to me, her ass jumping, her feet skittering. Cinderella drops down onto all fours across the street and into another alley. Even though my breath runs short and my chest burns, I follow her. I doubt the police are still on my tail. Who wants to arrest a man who threw up at an art show that badly?

Cinderella's tail flips into the shadows and she disappears around a corner. I turn, and she sits on the ground, tiny grey arms bent so that her small pink hands lift a tinfoil wrapped and half eaten burger to her mouth. Her long teeth pick into the spoiled meat. She pulls at a small chunk and swallows it down. Her tongue smacks behind her teeth. Her pink tail rubs its ribs against the wall, and her thick grey body fills the alley so that I can no longer see around her. She looks at me with her large eyes, timid and dumb. Does she recognize me? It looks like she's become a street rat, fat off junk food garbage. Her nose twitches at me. My fingers fumble for the zipper on my bag. I know this probably isn't real, but if it is, it deserves a picture. Her eyes match mine. A cold stirs in my stomach, and my fingers stop. No she doesn't a picture. Wow. This is the first time I ever thought that. and I look over my shoulder, searching for any human shadows bending at the corner. Looking for that little Miss Shit Beetle, knowing that if I took a picture, she'll find it. She'll steal the memory.

What's the point of remembering things, if you have no one to show it to? Hording enough memories should have made me memorable. But it didn't, so what's the point, if someone else is going to steal all my best efforts?

Cinderella tramps toward me. She stands up on her hind legs, and she's more than a foot taller than my own head. The claws on her pink hands flash and slash toward my chest. Desperately they scrape my coat away, tearing at my shirt. They shred through my clothes to my bare skin, and then she does the same for my pants, and the same for my shoes. Her tiny claws cut through everything, and they leave me standing naked in the alley. It's the first time I've been naked since I can remember. I wonder what she plans on doing. Does she want to have sex with me? I don't know how I feel about making love to a rat-girl who's also so fat and under age.

I wonder, if I tried to be her father when she wanted me to, would she have turned out the same?

She turns and runs off. I try to follow her, but her thick thighs kick dust and pebbles at me, and she pushes herself forward faster than my legs can keep up. Anyhow, my chest pounds, and my calves ache. I'm tired. I lose her as we break out from an alley into an open sidewalk, with the subway line overlooking the river. We're on the edge of the city, where a few white dots in the sky throw silver coins onto the ripples of water. My breath goes from my chest. I pace to the railing that protects the river and stare across to where factories and docks line the horizon. I've been so deep in the dark, entrenched in the buildings, in the alleys, in the dumpsters, the penthouses, and the filth, that I haven't been able to look out across the river since I was a kid. I unzip my bag and lift my camera. I lift the viewfinder to my eye, and I snap a single shot. Just a few silver waves and dots of light from the buildings along the background. I tap the screen for the last picture I took, but nothing comes up. I tap it again. Nothing. The screen reads one picture out of one. A tear drips off my nose, touches my lips. She has them. She really does has them all.

I drop the camera.

The river swallows it. I think of jumping in after it, of following it down, of grabbing it and bringing it back to the surface, but I'm not that dramatic; I'm not a psychopath. I slip the bag off my shoulder, pull out my mic and drop it in as well. I don't need to snap photos; I don't need to record voices. I just need eyes and ears and a mind no soul can tap into. I have all my memories, and they're all mine. And maybe if I remember enough of things, I can forget who I am. I can become the walls, the streets, the statues in the city. Or I can even become the city. I can become the mind of the city. And everyone will know me, because I'll be everywhere around them. I don't need to be someone. I need to become no one to the point that I cease to exist the way that other people do, until I exist like I'm a street lamp or a flock of birds. Until I become the menaquinones in the stores, the models on the walls. Something that everyone sees but no one sees. . That's what I want. It's something I've already been so good at, so close to, but I've been trying too hard to run in the opposite direction. I just need to stop running. I just need to let myself be, until I cease to be.

Finally, I let out a sigh, and I realize that I'm feeling proud of myself. Trying to be someone wasn't really me. I think I'll fit in more with this new persona. I watch myself smile into the water.

I've been training for this my whole life, the hiding, the lurking, the blending in. It was that need to record, to photograph, to remember, that got me all caught up. When I was doing it as a pure thing, as a boy, like if I saw breasts. I really just wanted to see those breasts again. And I wanted to feel the way I did when I saw them for the first time. Now I realized that what I wanted was to be ignored, to be left behind, just the way my mom left me. That's what she was really doing, training me. So thank you Mom, I won't let you down.

A large shadow pulls down the road to my side. I imagine it's little Miss Shit Beetle ready to take whatever's left of me. I'm ready to turn to her and to tell her she's going to be disappointed, that there's nothing left to take of me. I'm already no one. But that thought stops the second I see the holster hanging from the figure's hip.

"Hey," the officer shouts. "Stop right there!"

Goddamn, they're persistent.

I turn on my heels as his partner turns the corner and jumps out of their car, and they both dash after me.

My arms pump, hair bends, chest strains. In the distance, a figure of white flickers. A spectral arm bends down an alleyway, motioning toward me. As I move closer, I see the fingers curl, the details of their nails. They are black with white swirls. I turn the corner, and a body of white flesh, almost see-through to her organs and skull, opens her arms to me. She's bald, but I know the face, the smile. She falls in toward the wall of the alley.

"Jennifer," I whisper, surprised.

Her head starts to fade into the crusted brick. But her arms still stand out for me to embrace her.

"Hold me," she whispers back. "Hold onto me."

I move toward her and fall forward against the wall. My arms open wide, hands open, and they clasp her fingers, wind rushing through them. The feeling of her is cold like dew. I close my eyes and rest the side of my face against hers. The officers run past us, shouting for me to come out.

"Hold me," she whispers. "Come to me."

I stand with my face pressed to the brick, hands groping the stone. I know she's gone; she was never here. But maybe if I keep on my new path. If I slink and skulk, if I learn to bend my body like a cat's, if my body blends into the background like black fur against black shadow, if I become the walls and the streets, I can be swallowed by this city like that part of Jennifer that remains, and I will be able to find her again. Maybe this time I can have the courage to hold onto her.

I breathe into the wall, and I smell the thick musk of the city. I hold it in my lungs for as long as I can before sighing it free. The sun warms my back like it warms the steel and concrete around me. A smile pulls against my lips. The first one I've known in ages.

I am the wall. I am the sidewalk. I am the street. I am the lamps and the lights. I am the buildings and the cars. I am the dust. I am the ash. I am garbage and waste. I have become nothing, so that I can become everything.

One of the men in uniform paces past the alley. His heels pound a stop, and he turns. He squints, peers straight at me. I freeze. I'm sure he'll shout, point at my junk, remind me that I'm naked. He twists his neck, turns his head. Behind me, a pigeon stands on a paper bag, pecking down to where a rat scurries inside, flicking its tail out the opening. The man watches the bird, pulls his dark coat straight on his shoulders, and he walks away. My eyes follow him as he disappears into the morning fog, and I smile to myself. So far so good.